"You must be the one they sent away… Eros," Priya breathed, almost afraid that she was correct in her assumption.

"In the flesh." His lips smoothed into a perfect smile as the word fell silkily from his lips. "It seems my family did not manage to completely erase me from their history."

"Unfortunately not."

"That's an impressive skill you have." He sat forward, bracing his hands on his knees. "I almost feel the chill of your disapproval in the air."

"You expect me to be pleased that I'm being kidnapped on my wedding day?"

"Such dramatics." His brows raised, one hand pressing in the center of his chest. "What possible reason would I have to necessitate kidnapping you?"

Priya kept her features impassive, not entirely sure how to interpret her situation. Whatever his reasons for getting her alone this way, her gut told her that it was not good.

"I'll admit my intentions are not so noble. But I assure you, I have no need to steal you away. I have every confidence that once you know the truth behind your perfect groom…you will walk away all by yourself."

The Greeks' Race to the Altar

Claiming their legacy...or their wives?

The Mytikas family has long been surrounded by secrets and legend. Even in death, patriarch Zeus has every intention of making sure it stays that way.

He leaves one final challenge to his three would-be heirs... The one who makes it down the aisle first will inherit *everything*!

The race is on for these Greek billionaires—but soon it's about so much more than fulfilling the terms of the will... It's about claiming their convenient brides!

Discover Eros's story in
Stolen in Her Wedding Gown
Available now!

And look out for Xander's and Nysio's stories
Coming soon!

Amanda Cinelli

STOLEN IN HER WEDDING GOWN

HARLEQUIN
PRESENTS

HARLEQUIN®
PRESENTS®

Recycling programs
for this product may
not exist in your area.

ISBN-13: 978-1-335-40368-1

Stolen in Her Wedding Gown

For questions and comments about the quality of this book,
please contact us at CustomerService@Harlequin.com.

Harlequin Enterprises ULC
22 Adelaide St. West, 40th Floor
Toronto, Ontario M5H 4E3, Canada
www.Harlequin.com

Printed in U.S.A.

Amanda Cinelli was born into a large Irish Italian family and raised in the leafy-green suburbs of County Dublin, Ireland. After dabbling in a few different career paths, she finally found her calling as an author upon winning an online writing competition with her first finished novel. With three small daughters at home, she usually spends her days doing school runs, changing diapers and writing romance. She still considers herself unbelievably lucky to be able to call this her day job.

Books by Amanda Cinelli

Harlequin Presents

Resisting the Sicilian Playboy

Secret Heirs of Billionaires

The Secret to Marrying Marchesi

Monteverre Marriages

One Night with the Forbidden Princess
Claiming His Replacement Queen

The Avelar Family Scandals

The Vows He Must Keep
Returning to Claim His Heir

Visit the Author Profile page
at Harlequin.com for more titles.

For Sarah

The best friend a girl could ask for.

CHAPTER ONE

EROS THEODOROU RAISED the single glass of ouzo into the air and made a silent toast to the night sky above his Athens penthouse. His mother stood by his side, a haunted darkness in her eyes as she stared out into nothing.

'I didn't expect you to play the grieving widow.' He placed his glass down on the ledge with unnecessary force, not bothering to mask his irritation.

'I may not legally be his widow…but I loved him.' Arista sighed, turning to face him with a hint of steel in her pale grey eyes. 'I was with him until the end.'

The thought of his formidable mother playing nursemaid, kneeling once again to the whims of such a man…it was enough to make Eros see red. The world knew Arista Theodorou for two things, her powerful career as legal adviser to the global elite and her disastrous on-again-off-again relationship with Zeus Mytikas.

'The bastard always knew how to manipulate you.' Eros cursed swiftly under his breath and felt his fists tighten as an old darkness threatened to resurface—the resentment and hatred that he'd long ago learned to keep buried.

'You didn't come to the memorial,' Arista said, her tone laced with disapproval.

Still pulling strings from beyond the grave, the old man had arranged for his body to be returned to his home country. Over the past week, it seemed the entire capital city had turned out in mourning for their most powerful ex-citizen. Eros felt his lip curl in revulsion. 'If I wished to attend a public spectacle, I'd go to the circus.'

'He was your father.'

Her cool hand touched his forearm, a rare show of affection. He allowed himself a moment to savour the novelty before calmly removing it.

'*No.* He wasn't.'

The taut syllables seemed to sit in the air between them, silently daring his mother to contest his words. As he expected, she averted her gaze. Eros had long ago learned that the title of father was one that needed to be earned. The blood that connected him to Zeus was only that. A genetic link that could not be erased, no matter how much money or power he amassed.

'Why are you here, Mother?'

'Our schedules never seem to have us in the

same city at the same time…' she said quickly, avoiding his eyes as she touched the small briefcase at her feet. 'I thought we might have dinner… Talk.'

'The truth.' Eros rolled his eyes, despising the use of niceties to conceal hidden motives. With Arista, there was always a hidden motive.

'Fine.' All traces of kindness vanished from her eyes. 'There are some urgent matters that we must discuss.'

'Make it quick, I have a date in half an hour.'

'Of course you do.' His mother's expression tightened. 'You talk of his philandering ways, and yet—'

'If you finish that sentence you can show yourself out,' Eros warned.

'I didn't mean to touch a nerve.' Arista shrugged, her tone flat and lacking its usual bite.

'If you must know, unlike your darling Zeus, I actually respect the women I entertain. They are quite aware that I am not in the habit of long-term arrangements, so there are no misunderstandings or accusations. It's called communication, Mother, you should try it.'

'Are you really so arrogant as to believe you haven't broken women's hearts simply because you told them not to give them to you?' Arista scoffed, lifting a slim black folder from the depths of her designer handbag.

Any retort to her words was lost as Eros eyed the official documents, a dull roar building in his ears. 'What is this?'

'Zeus's last will and testament.'

He remained deathly still, controlling the violent reaction that boiled in his veins. 'You have got to be joking.'

He leaned against the balcony edge, a harsh bellow of laughter escaping his chest. 'After he tried to ruin my businesses, after the threats and reminders that I walked away from leading his empire…'

Disbelief warred with rage within him as he tried to focus on the sweeping view over the city that stretched all the way to the Acropolis. He was vaguely aware of his mother as she heaved a sigh and took a seat beside him. Her dark blond hair was identical to his own, a feature he'd always been grateful for as it put him another step away from the sleek black darkness of the powerful Mytikas family. He was not easily recognised as one of them, even if his cerulean blue eyes were a permanent reminder of the man who'd done the bare minimum in contributing to his birth.

Eros sat back, kicking his heels up onto the table in front of him. 'Let me guess, he had a change of heart and decided to leave everything to me and nothing to his other by-blows.'

Arista stiffened at the reminder that she was not the only woman to produce an illegitimate child by one of the wealthiest men in the world.

'It's not quite that simple.' She shook her head. 'There are stipulations…'

'Look around.' He gestured to the penthouse suite that sat atop the high-rise tower he owned in the centre of Athens's financial district. 'Why would I want to take his poisonous empire when I've built one of my own? I have no need to jump through his hoops.'

He was merely the second born of three bastard sons that Zeus had chosen to acknowledge in his lifetime. The image of Xander's face came unbidden into his mind and he pushed it away. His traitorous half-brother had made it clear where his loyalties stood the moment he took Zeus's name and stepped into the role of prodigal son.

As for the third and youngest of their merry trio, a reclusive member of one of the oldest dynasties in Italy, Nysio Bacchetti had made it impossible for anyone to connect his powerful family name with that of his hidden paternal link.

'This stipulation…it applies to all three of us?' Eros fought to keep his tone even. 'What have the others had to say on the matter?'

Arista shook her head. 'The Italian didn't even

answer my calls. He will not risk the link being made public. But Xander has long known what he stood to lose if Zeus changed his mind… mainly his majority shareholder position and his place as acting CEO.'

He took the documents from his mother's hands and read through the highlighted text. Silence descended upon them and he could feel his mother's anxious gaze.

The first to remain in a valid marriage for one year, inherits all.

The words settled like lead in his gut. Marriage? He had walked away from Zeus's fiercely traditional values and control, but he had to admit that attempting to enforce matrimony from beyond the grave was an impressive feat.

'So Xander knows about this?'

'He knows…and he is already engaged. No announcement in the paper, no engagement party, it's all been kept completely under wraps.'

'Very convenient,' Eros murmured, still skimming down the legal pages spread out before him. Sure enough, the document made clear that of the three illegitimate sons Zeus had fathered, whoever married first and completed the terms would take everything. He sat back in his seat, tension building in his temples.

'Eros, don't you see…he's already acting like he has won. Our last board meeting was dominated by talk of his plans to purge the company of excess.' Arista's voice turned cold. 'He made it clear that my position in the company would fall under that category.'

He turned to his mother, fire in his veins and all thoughts of his date firmly forgotten. 'This conversation is futile. You know that I will never marry.'

'Not even to spite Xander?' Her voice raised an octave as she continued. 'I need to retain control at Mytikas and the only way I can achieve that is with my own son at the helm. Please, Eros.'

He saw her expression soften and knew this was a part of her act. It was always this way with Arista. For such a powerhouse of a woman, he had often seen her reduce herself to theatrics to achieve her goals. She would promise the stars, only to walk away once she had got what she needed.

He thought of his childhood spent watching her manipulate the one man who had loved her for the one who never would. His stepfather, a proud man who'd craved a simple family life, had died expecting her to change. Once upon a time, Eros had expected her to change too.

He turned to stare out at the starlit sky, his mind struggling to remain on track, as it often did with sudden shifts of information. Decades overcoming an embarrassingly inconvenient childhood stammer made him hyperaware of moments that might trigger a relapse. His jaw tightened and he carefully inhaled and exhaled a breath before speaking, just in case.

'What do you expect me to do? Barge into the church and object? Surely you can do that yourself.'

'I can't risk my position, you know that. Plus... If we want to make sure this marriage doesn't go ahead, it's not just the ceremony that needs to be ruined.'

'Ah... I see.' He forced his tone to remain calm, not belying the flash of anger that seethed in his veins. 'You don't just need my help, Mother. You need my reputation.'

'I need this bride to become suddenly, irrevocably unmarriageable. At the very least, it will give me time to contest the will. If you are determined not to fulfil it yourself.'

'I must admit, the thought of ruining Xander's perfectly laid plans is quite tempting,' Eros mused, running a hand along his jaw.

'Will you do it or not?' Arista snapped, her loss of patience sudden and sharp against the stillness of the night air. 'I just...want your brother to pay for how he betrayed you. I don't want him to win.'

Eros felt his fists tighten at her impatience, knowing that his mother had never once tried to stand up for her only son in the past. She had remained at Zeus's beck and call while Eros had gone out into the world, using nothing but rage and bitterness to forge his way alone.

The memories remained under the surface of his control but he drew upon the emotion they evoked as he stood up and took his mother's hands in his own. He saw her eyes light up with barely restrained hope.

It was rather poetic that her fatal error would so perfectly mirror that of the man she'd loved so much. Arista believed him weak, just as Zeus had, but now she was unwittingly inviting a ravenous wolf into the hencoop.

'Rest easy. I will stop the wedding.'

'You will?' she said hopefully. 'And the bride?'

'Consider her already taken care of.' He kept his features neutral. 'You just focus on contesting the will. I will do the rest.'

'This deal remains confidential between us?' she said sharply. 'If I succeed, the house in the Hamptons and the seat on the board will be mine but everything else is yours for the taking.'

'Of course,' he said silkily. 'Have I ever given you a reason not to trust me?'

Her expression softened, her objective met,

and she sipped on her own ouzo like a cat who had just got the proverbial cream.

It was only once she had gone and Eros was alone with the stars once more that he allowed the ghost of a smile to touch his lips. Using his phone, he searched for the name of the woman his mother had given him before she'd left. His brother's bride.

He had long imagined what he might do if he ever got the opportunity to seek revenge on those who had wronged him…but he had never considered there might be collateral damage. He would go to New York and he would destroy his brother's plot and ensure that in a matter of weeks there would be no Mytikas Holdings for them to fight over.

He would destroy everything. Divide it up and sell it off piece by piece.

He looked at the photo on his phone once again, running his finger across the image. His big brother had chosen a pretty bride. He wondered if the beauty knew of the world she was entering into. Even if she didn't, he could not allow himself to feel guilt. It wasn't his fault if his brother had drawn an innocent into the crossfire.

In this family…all was fair in love and war.

'What do you think you're doing?'

Priya Davidson Khan jolted upright in her

seat at the sound of her best friend's voice in the doorway of the office, her surprise causing her to knock over the neat stack of documents she'd been studying. 'I had a few things that needed my attention.'

'On a Sunday?' Aria strode into the room and stopped to glare down at her with obvious disdain. 'Don't you have somewhere rather important to be?'

'Money never sleeps,' Priya grumbled, furiously gathering the scrambled pile of pages. After another sleepless night, she'd come into the deserted office to calm herself by double-checking the most up-to-date figures for the company she would soon own. She'd set her plan in motion, lining up all the various parts she required until her inheritance finally became her own. She just needed to survive the next few hours first…

'Step away from the spreadsheets.' Her friend's feet appeared in her peripheral vision as she scooped up more of the errant papers under the vast mahogany desk.

Priya looked up, properly taking in the extravagant dusty pink bridesmaid's gown that Aria wore and the long white garment bag in her hands.

Her stomach sank as she took in the elegant black script on the front that read Bride.

'Sweetheart…if you were planning to run from a wedding again, you could have chosen somewhere a little more glamorous.' Aria smiled good-naturedly.

Priya swallowed hard, feeling her anxiety peak at that single word.

Again.

Her best friend wasn't trying to be cruel. They often joked of her disastrous first engagement and the society scandal that had come from her abrupt departure mere hours before the ceremony. But that had been in the past, when she'd believed herself free of this world with all its expectations and power plays. She pushed away the sinking feeling of dread and stood up, wiping down her moist palms on her tailored black suit trousers.

'What time is it?'

'Just past two.' Aria's expression softened as she stepped into the office suite and closed the double doors softly behind her. Frustration she could have dealt with, but the look of kind concern on Aria's pretty face was too much.

'Are you *sure* you want to go through with this? With…him?'

Priya thought of the *him* her friend referred to and felt the urge to growl that of course she wasn't sure. Xander Mytikas had been a last-minute choice, a deal brokered by her uncle as part of their family's desperate bid to avoid ruin. Where else was she going to find a temporary husband willing to walk away from a woman of her fortune without demanding a pay-out?

She had met the powerful financier for dinner a few times over the week before, and he had his own reasons for their arrangement, which suited her just fine. There was no attraction between them, no risk of complications. So why did she still feel this stifling sense of suffocation every time she thought of their agreement?

Perhaps it was the two-page newspaper spread he had already ordered to announce their union once it was made public, a small voice whispered inside her. She pushed the thoughts of the media away, feeling her anxiety climb. Of course the news of his wishes for a public marriage had come as a shock. Who wanted to take part in a society marriage after publicly proclaiming their lifelong spinsterhood to the world? She could already imagine the headlines.

Let them call her a social climber, let them focus on the scandal…no one could know the truth behind her hasty nuptials.

'Just help me get this on, please?' Priya exhaled a long breath and took the garment bag from her friend's hands, avoiding her questioning gaze as she undid the zip and revealed the extravagant white gown that had been selected by the top stylist in charge of the event. That was how she'd thought of it in her head until this moment, a nameless event to tick off on her weekly agenda. Only now, feeling the silk under her fingertips, she felt the first rumblings of panic under the smooth facade of her infamous ice-queen composure.

The closure of tiny hooks and buttons threatened to cut off her circulation and she'd barely caught a glimpse of her reflection smothered in expensive white silk before she forced herself to look away.

'Could you go ahead to the ceremony and tell them I'm running late?' Priya avoided her friend's eyes. 'I just…need a moment.'

Aria embraced her in a quick hug, her mouth opening but then closing on whatever words she had wished to say. With one last frown, she closed the doors behind her and Priya let out a shuddering breath. On unsteady feet, she looked around her at what had once been Arun Davidson Khan's domain. The last piece left of her father's legacy.

The New York headquarters of Davidson Khan Financial was all that remained of what had once been an international empire. The building was a slice of gilded history and had always been a favourite haunt of hers with its grand vaulted ceilings and unrivalled views of the Hudson in the distance through the sash windows.

Remembering what she'd always done as a girl, she placed her hands on the cool glass and listened to the hum of the city, trying to draw the white noise into herself to block out the chaos of her thoughts. All too soon she forced herself to move backwards, back towards the private elevator that would take her down to her fate.

Like a woman on her way to the gallows, she clamped her hands by her sides, mentally preparing to take the first step back into the flames she'd spent seven years escaping.

New York society was vicious at the best of times, but to the heiress who had publicly spurned it… She would never know true peace again.

As a young girl growing up amongst Long Island's elite, Priya remembered planning her fairy-tale wedding day with her friends. With a silk scarf for a veil and an illicitly obtained bouquet from Mama's prized rose garden, she would imagine herself to be a grand society bride just like her perfectly polished mother had been.

But it turned out her mother had been far from perfect, and her love had only ever been conditional upon Priya doing as she was told and following the rules expected of an upper-class heiress.

For seven years, she had taken time to just be herself. But once she got married…she would be a billionaire.

Closing her eyes tightly, she fought to inhale, but every attempt seemed to only serve to tighten the bands forming around her ribcage.

The private elevator came to a stop far too quickly for her liking and as the doors opened into the empty executive atrium, her path was blocked by a broad figure in a sleek black suit. She was momentarily transfixed by a pair of cerulean blue eyes framed by the kind of angular bone structure and full lips that were usually reserved for the catwalk.

For a long, ridiculous moment all she could do was stare. *Beauty* was not a word often used to describe men…but there was no other word to accurately encompass the *force* of viewing such a face. His dark blond hair was pulled back into a neat style, but she could tell that it would fall almost to his shoulders unbound. Coupled with the perfectly groomed shadow of stubble along his jawline, the overall effect gave him a rather dangerous quality that seemed quite at odds with the serene smile on his lips. As though he'd heard her thoughts, that smile tilted up to one side and his features were transformed anew.

'You must be the bride.' His voice was deep and slightly accented.

Priya's heart thumped against her breastbone and she swallowed hard, her throat suddenly parched even as she pressed her lips flat and reminded herself that she was not a swooning teenager. She *was* the bride and she was currently late to her own wedding.

'Did the white dress give me away?' she asked tartly.

'I think it was the overwhelming aura of excitement,' he replied, copying her tone.

A dimple appeared in one of his cheeks and she studiously ignored it, focusing on the slim white access card in his hands, a card that was only given to security guards or drivers.

'I didn't order a car.' She frowned; she hadn't even thought of it. 'Xander really did think of everything.'

Something briefly darkened in his gaze but the smile on his face remained intact as he opened the doors that led to the rear street access of the building. He turned, tipping his head to one side. 'Do you need assistance with the gown?'

'I'll manage,' she said stiffly, not knowing why his innocent attention felt discomfiting, and not entirely appropriate. He was handsome, but she had met countless handsome men during the years she had worked abroad in foreign investment firms. She had never exactly gravitated to any of them but, still, she noticed.

She was about to get married to one of the most powerful men in New York and she was being distracted by some very inappropriate thoughts for her *chauffeur*.

They emerged into the gloomy autumn drizzle and she was suddenly grateful for the broad male shoulders that shielded her from view of curious pedestrians as they passed under the canopy to where a long silver limousine waited.

Huffing out a breath, she tried to slide gracefully onto the butter-soft leather seat but only succeeded in falling in very slowly. How women were expected to move freely in these ridiculous haute couture creations was completely beyond her. If it had been up to her, she'd be saying her vows in something far more functional.

Without comment, the driver leaned down and rearranged the silk, which had been trailing towards the wet ground, carefully around her feet. The angle of his head made her stiffen, her body tingling with what she hoped was just nerves. When he finally straightened and closed the door, she could breathe. What on earth had got into her?

She may not be in an actual romantic relationship with her groom but she had promised that she would play the perfect society bride. That meant maintaining the appearance of a blissfully married couple for the next year. She had no need for such a lengthy time frame, but Xander had insisted. There could be no scandal, no accusations of a staged union. It needed to look real.

Twelve months was a small price to pay to unlock her inheritance. As much as she hated it, she had grown up a part of this world so she could easily play the part of the blushing bride for a time. It was no big deal, really...

Closing her eyes tightly, she focused on her breathing and the sound of the engine being brought to life, so much so that she missed the sound of the opposite door opening and closing quickly, before the car began to move.

'Champagne?'

Her thoughts interrupted by that smooth accented voice, her eyes snapped open to find she was not alone and she jolted back in her seat.

'Who on earth is driving the car?' She shook her head, feeling the very definite sensation of the vehicle beginning to move.

'The driver, of course.'

Priya felt her mouth slacken with dismay as her surprise guest nonchalantly pressed a button to reveal two chilled flutes and a bottle of expensive champagne.

'You...you deliberately misled me.' She sat up straighter in her seat, realising with a sharp tug of horror that she'd been so distracted she'd left without alerting the security guard that had been assigned to her.

'I never said that I was your driver.' His eyes had that same amused glow again, as though he found the situation highly entertaining.

'Who are you and why are you here?' She narrowed her gaze.

'I'm here to talk to you, of course.' Strong golden-skinned hands carefully popped the stopper and poured. 'I've been told I resemble a fallen angel. Maybe today I'm yours.'

She deliberately ignored the glass he offered her.

'That's not an answer.' She slipped her phone out of her small handbag and gave him her best glare. 'You have ten seconds to tell me your purpose here before I call the police.'

'What will you tell them, Priya?' he said silkily, his exotic accent seeming to caress each syllable as they passed his lips. 'What kind of terrible things are you imagining I might do to you? I'm curious.'

Her skin instantly prickled with gooseflesh. Who on earth was this man and why did everything he say sound like a lover's bedroom whispers? Tightening her fists, she tried and failed to conceal the sudden tremor in her body.

'Relax, princess. You are not in danger from me.' He exhaled sharply, as though her reaction had deeply irritated him. Without breaking eye contact, he reached across to press a small button on the side panel. 'You recognise Ennio, yes?'

The screen behind him was lowered and Priya felt her chest ease slightly as she took in the kind face of the man who had chauffeured her around the city many times in the past weeks. His smile held a hint of guilt as he waved once and raised the screen again, leaving her alone with her mystery guest once more.

'Did you bribe my driver?' she asked.

'*Bribe* is such an ugly word, don't you think?' He slung one powerful arm along the back of the seat, surveying her over the rim of his glass. 'I prefer to think of it as…offering a preferable incentive.'

'Who are you?' she repeated with as much steel as she could muster, considering the thousand butterflies currently using her stomach as a cage.

'You mean he didn't tell you about me?' He feigned being wounded in the centre of his chest, tutting softly. 'Seems my brother is hiding more from you than just his true motive behind this marriage. You're lucky I'm here to set the balance right before you make it down the aisle.'

His *brother*. Priya felt her mouth open slightly before she closed it again. Being part of New York society, it was impossible not to know about her groom's powerful father and his infamous indiscretions but nothing about the man in front of her was anything like her finely polished and serious fiancé. Xander was dark and lean where this man was golden-skinned and had shoulders that seemed to fill the entire seat. His collar was open and his long golden hair brushed back in the kind of effortless style that only looked good on a man of his calibre. He practically oozed sex appeal and vitality, so much so that she forced herself to look away from his knowing gaze and remind herself of what was at stake.

She knew that Xander had ulterior motives that he hadn't revealed but she had ensured that their prenuptial agreement was ironclad. She'd read through the papers herself, their arrangement was crystal clear. Everything was under control.

'You're clearly here to make a revelation of some sort, so kindly get to it. I'm already running late.' She smoothed her hands down flat in her lap, gathering her expression into a cool mask.

'Do you love him?'

'That's…none of your business,' she responded tautly, her jaw tightening with barely restrained irritation. As though he hadn't got the answer he wanted, her mysterious guest simply frowned and took another slow sip of champagne.

'I've seen the prenuptial agreement…you certainly have a routine mapped out. Dinners in public, social events… You seem quite eager to bolster your reputation now that you've returned to society.'

'You don't know me.' Priya spoke through clenched teeth.

'I know enough.' He downed the remnants of his champagne in one movement, the golden liquid glittering for a moment on his lips. 'I know that one sordid photograph with me would be all it takes for my brother to discard you and whatever deal you've made.'

Priya fought past the sudden dryness in her throat, hardly able to process such a scandalous threat. 'What benefit could possibly come from ruining this wedding in such a dramatic way?'

'Oh, no, princess… I'm not just here to ruin the wedding.' He leaned forward, his full lips stretching into a sinful smirk. 'I'm here to ruin *you*.'

CHAPTER TWO

'YOU ARE THE one Xander was worried about.' The realisation hit her with sudden clarity as she remembered a conversation she'd overheard as they'd navigated the complicated terms of their prenuptial agreement.

There are members of my family who may pose a problem.

She'd heard mention of her fiancé's feuding Greek family but she hadn't taken them too seriously. She took in the man seated across from her once more, this time seeing his ethereal beauty for what it was. A colourful trap designed to lure a woman to her doom.

'You must be the one they sent away... Eros.' She breathed deeply, almost afraid that she was correct in her assumption. She'd only ever heard whispers of Eros Theodorou, a powerful Greek investment banker and property mogul. His reputation amongst the elite of Europe was one of the work hard, play hard variety.

'In the flesh.' His lips smoothed into a perfect smile as the word fell silkily from his lips. 'It seems my family did not manage to completely erase me from their history.'

'Unfortunately not.'

'That's an impressive skill you have.' He sat forward, bracing his hands on his knees. 'I almost feel the chill of your disapproval in the air.'

'You expect me to be pleased that I'm being kidnapped on my wedding day?'

'Such dramatics.' His brows rose as one hand pressed against the centre of his chest. 'What possible reason would I have to necessitate kidnapping you?'

Priya kept her features impassive, not entirely sure how to interpret her situation. Whatever his reasons for getting her alone this way, her gut told her that it was not good.

'For all you know, my plan is to simply escort you to your handsome groom myself.' He spoke with thinly veiled amusement.

'There would be no need for theatrics if that was the case.' She raised one brow.

'True.' He tilted his glass in her direction. 'I'll admit my intentions are not so noble. But I assure you I have no need to steal you away. I have every confidence that once you know the truth behind this rather sudden union, you will walk away all by yourself.'

'You're despicable.' She exhaled sharply.

'Believe it or not, I'm the least of your problems.' He looked impressively villainous all of a sudden, watching her from the shadows. 'I'm simply here to serve a warning that this family thrives on deception.'

'You expect me to heed a warning from you?' she said tautly, feeling her nails dig into her palms. 'I read that you were caught selling company secrets. You're a criminal.'

'So the stories say.' He sighed with an air of boredom.

'So that's not true?'

'I don't know what amuses me more, that people believe me a white-collar criminal or that they believe I allowed myself to get caught.'

'You find it funny to have your reputation precede you?'

'Do you?' His eyes seemed to turn a shade darker as his gaze momentarily caught on the large diamond ring on her finger. 'Does my brother know about what happened to your last groom?'

His words hit her square in the chest and she fought to regain her composure for a long moment. 'Do you have to practise being so offensive or does it come naturally?'

'It's one of my many talents.' He sat forward, his cerulean eyes meeting hers with such intensity she fought not to squirm. 'So, let's get to the point. Did your uncle force you into this little marriage bargain of yours or did you offer yourself up willingly?'

Priya narrowed her eyes, feeling her heartbeat quicken. 'Why would I satisfy you with an answer to such a ridiculous question?'

'I've done my research, Miss Davidson Khan.' He tilted his head to one side, studying her with quiet focus. 'For one of the wealthiest heiresses in the country, you have been living a rather modest lifestyle. You're on track to come into your inheritance in three years, so you have no pressing reasons to enter into such a bargain. Your uncle, on the other hand...'

He flipped open the case of a slim tablet computer by his side and it sprang to life, filled with rows upon rows of numbers. Priya feigned nonchalance as she peered closer, praying it wasn't what it seemed to be. Praying that he was bluffing.

He was not.

'How did you get access to this?' she asked in shock.

'Let's just say it's a talent of mine, hunting down secrets that powerful people wish to keep hidden from the world.' He snapped the case shut, making her jump. 'A wealth management firm with a CEO secretly drowning in debt. Quite a headline, don't you think?'

'Is that what this is? You're here to blackmail me on my wedding day?' She felt anger rise within her at his serene expression as he remained silent, slowly swirling his index finger around the rim of his champagne flute.

He continued. 'I was just curious why you would wait so long to inherit the shares in your father's company, only to hand them over in a buyout.'

'I have not agreed to a buyout.'

'Are you sure about that?'

His words held no amusement now as he drew up another file for her perusal, the contract that she had signed days before. Only now her uncle's signature had been added, along with one particular amendment. Xander Mytikas was vying for a merger…and Vikram planned to give it to him.

Blue eyes watched her, his full lips pressed into a hard line. 'My brother has a poor track record when it comes to promises. And your uncle has already proved where his loyalties lie.'

Priya felt her thoughts swirl out of control, the pressure of the past week finally threatening to overwhelm her. This was too much. From the moment she had agreed to this ridiculous marriage bargain, she had inwardly fought against it.

She had walked away from this life seven years
ago for a reason and now she was being dragged
back into it kicking and screaming.

She didn't have to save her uncle; she could
leave him to his own fate. But would she ever
forgive herself if she let the last of her father's
beloved company disappear, absorbed into some
faceless conglomerate? She'd promised that she
would make him proud. She'd vowed to carry
out the plans he'd begun, once she had gathered
enough experience to earn her place.

'I've already agreed to the deal. Even if this is
all true…' She shook her head, frustration and
anxiety making her pull and fuss with the folds
of silk that swamped her. 'I suppose you are here
to warn me out of the goodness of your own
heart?'

'Of course not.'

'Then why?' she urged. 'Revenge?'

'Something like that, yes.' His eyes turned
dark with a flash of malice, his gaze moving to
look out the window.

'Quite a theatrical notion for a self-professed
villain. Why on earth should I trust you?'

'You shouldn't.' He ran strong fingers along
his jaw. 'Someone as wealthy as you stand to become should trust no one. Especially not people
who place conditions on their false concern.'

'Ah, so your concern is genuine?'

'I don't make a habit of caring for the plight of small investment firms that are utterly irrelevant to my business interests.' He met her gaze, no trace of remorse on his beautiful features. 'I can offer you something else. Freedom.'

'I am free. I chose to accept this deal with my eyes open. Despite your flattering appraisal, I am not some damsel in distress in need of rescue.'

'I am not here to rescue you. The single term of my offer is simple,' he interjected smoothly. 'Walk away from this wedding. Publicly. Abandon my brother and his precious image…and I will buy your father's company myself and hand it to you, no strings attached.'

'Revenge would be worth that much to you?'

'My brother once caused me a great deal of public shame and ridicule. I can think of no situation more perfect for him.'

Priya sucked in a sharp breath, unable to look away from that dark smile on his lips. How could a man with such striking beauty be so cold and calculating? She closed her eyes briefly, feeling her pulse thrumming in her ears. How had she got into this situation where she was tempted by such an unlikely escape?

The man she'd agreed to marry had a reputation for being ruthless in the boardroom, true, but he had never given her reason to mistrust him. Still, thoughts arose, memories of his evasion of her questions behind his motives. He would only say that he needed the marriage for his own private legal reasons.

The idea that Vikram had conspired to secretly force through a merger was not so farfetched. The only reason she'd even found out about his debts was because he'd been busily selling off all of his own shares. But Xander had seemed so earnest in his sympathy for her plight. Was it possible that she had once again completely misjudged a man claiming to have her best interests at heart?

Maybe he would be relieved if she called everything off...

Hearing the selfish direction of her thoughts, she mentally shook herself. No. She couldn't walk away from this...no matter how far out of her comfort zone she was. She had to at least speak to him first.

The car came to a sudden stop and Priya looked sideways, shocked to see that they had arrived at the courthouse already. Blue eyes remained trained on her, waiting for her answer to his offer.

Waiting for her to put her faith and the future of hundreds of employees into the hands of a stranger.

'I... I can't trust you. I'm sorry.'

Without waiting for assistance, she threw the

door open and used every ounce of strength she had to lift herself to a standing position and step carefully outside. The sidewalk was eerily empty and the grey stone building looked even more imposing under the murky grey clouds that blanketed the sky above them. There was a heaviness to the air, as though the heavens above were set to burst at any moment.

A cab careened to a stop nearby and she recognised the furious figure of her bodyguard emerging from the passenger seat. She shivered, looking back down to find Eros's lightening gaze still intensely focused upon her.

'Let me make this clear, this offer expires the moment you turn your back on me,' he warned darkly.

She took a step back and slowly turned, hearing a dark chuckle emerge from behind her. For a moment she wondered if Eros Theodorou was going to follow through on his threat to accompany her into her wedding ceremony himself. But moments later she heard the door being pulled shut with a final click.

The bodyguard came to a stop by her side, panting and agitated. 'Are you unharmed, Miss Davidson Khan?'

'I'm fine.' She pressed her lips into a thin line but inside she was furious at herself for making such a glaring lapse in judgement. She was the queen of details, she never missed a step. Yet with one mere flash of a charmer's smile, she'd gotten into a car with a stranger like a wayward child.

Squaring her shoulders, she resisted the urge to look back and began scaling the steep steps. It was unusually quiet for an afternoon in Manhattan.

Her thoughts threatened to consume her and drag her further away from the quiet, resolved demeanour she'd adapted in the past days. She was no longer able to ignore her roiling thoughts. Her calm sea had been ravaged by the storm that was Eros Theodorou.

She suddenly wished she hadn't been so intent on doing this alone. Perhaps this was why brides were walked into a wedding by their fathers, so that they were less likely to run.

But her father was dead and her mother was already inside with her uncle, watching to make sure she followed through on her promise to save them.

She wasn't just walking alone, she *was* alone. She was so distracted by her melancholy thoughts that she didn't see the cameras until the first flash blinded her. She halted mid-step, her gown forming a stark white cloud against the dark stone. As if in horrifying slow-motion, the entire platform at the top of the steps became swarmed with reporters.

Priya froze.

A couple dozen eyes fell upon her with laser focus. Pedestrians slowed down in her peripheral vision, craning their necks to get a good look at the spectacle she presented. A tableau of perfectly polished fear and uncertainty.

Just walk, she urged herself, feeling the panic rise in her throat. Fewer than ten steps separated her from clearing up the details of the prenup, unlocking her inheritance and saving her family's name from ruin. Just a few more steps and she would have done her duty to her father. She would be on the pathway to freedom.

But the crawling claws of fear grew inside her chest, making her feel like she was trapped underwater and being pulled downward. A quick look behind her revealed an empty space where the limousine had been. The knowledge that she was truly alone intensified her panic. Her lungs felt like they were filling with water with each second that passed. She needed to move. She needed to breathe.

One quick glance upward revealed her uncle pushing past the shoulders of the paparazzi and journalists who had overrun the courthouse entrance. Vikram moved towards her and she held up a hand to stop him.

'Did you amend the prenup?' she asked shakily, watching the immediate play of guilt and anger across his dark features.

'This is not the time or place to cause a scene, Priya,' he growled. 'Get inside.'

She immediately took a step back, out of his reach. 'Even after I came to save you, you still couldn't help yourself?' She shook her head with disbelief.

'The company is dead in the water anyway,' he hissed under his breath, eyes darting towards the reporters eagerly flashing their cameras. 'This way we all win.'

'How dare you.' She felt her legs begin to shake as she stumbled backwards, feeling the eyes of what seemed like a thousand onlookers follow her. A quick glance showed Xander emerging from the doorway, only to be blocked by a wall of people. He met her eyes, one dark brow rising in silent question, and Priya felt the final knot of indecision lock into place.

Shaking her head slowly, she tried to convey her apology without words. He may have been swayed by a bad deal with Vikram but no one deserved this kind of humiliation. She should never have agreed to their marriage in the first place.

As he realised her intention, his face hardened with concern and he seemed to try to push through the crowd. Priya didn't wait to see if he succeeded. She turned and fled down the remainder of the steps.

As she made quick progress down the street, the earlier mist suddenly gave way to a steady downpour. She felt her hair and shoulders become soaked instantly but had no time for vanity. Without her purse, which she had somehow dropped, she couldn't even hail a cab. The reality of her decision seemed to hit her with finality as she came to a stop in a narrow alleyway and felt a sob threaten to choke her.

Thinking of the humiliation she'd just caused made her throat clench painfully, so she forced herself to focus on how on earth she was going to navigate the streets of New York in pouring rain wearing a giant haute couture wedding gown.

As she tried to clear her mind and formulate a plan, a familiar sleek silver limousine appeared at the opposite end of the alleyway and came to an immediate stop. A tall, broad frame stepped out into the rain, blond hair darkening instantly under the heavy downpour.

Priya felt a shameful mixture of frustration and relief as she watched Eros move towards her with leonine grace.

'You're faster than I anticipated,' he said as he reached her side, his face strangely devoid of either triumph or judgement.

She hated the fact that he seemed so confi-

dent that she would run and that he had tracked
her with such ease. In the brief moments of their
meeting, he'd done his best to show her exactly
what he knew would make her want out of her ill-
fated deal. The knowledge made her fists tighten
with anger.

She was vaguely aware of a dark coat being
draped around her body, cocooning her in
warmth and the unusual scent of mint and sandalwood. She hesitated, unable to decide if, by
accepting his help, she was accepting everything
he had offered. She looked up, meeting his eyes
for the first time and feeling her stomach clench
at the intensity she saw there.

She may have just walked away from her best
chance of unlocking her trust fund and saving
the firm by herself, but if she was actually considering accepting an offer of no-strings help
from a man with his reputation, she had certainly
lost her mind.

'I just need to get out of here, please,' she
said with as much strength as she could muster, feeling the cold of the rain seeping into her
skin through his coat. The wedding gown was
a dead weight now, sodden and dark with mud
at the hem. She didn't care. She needed him to
know that just because she had run from the
wedding—just because she was getting into this
limo—it didn't mean she was trusting him.

Liar, something whispered deep within her.

'Your rescue comes at a price.' His words were tight with what sounded like irritation. 'But we can discuss that once we're somewhere less wet and freezing.'

What happened to no strings? she thought with sudden anger. Did all men believe that they could simply change the rules on a whim?

Before she could challenge him, a buzz of voices sounded out behind them and Priya turned her head just as a bulb flashed brightly in her face, momentarily blinding her.

A growl, low and feral, came from her side and she was lifted over one powerful shoulder. He moved fast down the alley, his face a mask of calm as he dropped her unceremoniously into the darkness of the limousine interior, the door closing with a sharp thud behind her.

Through the tinted glass, she watched as Eros loomed over the small group of photographers that had pursued her like dogs on a blood trail. His threats were dark and muffled by the window, but effective considering the crowd seemed to shrink away immediately. The door opened and he slid in with ease, taking the seat directly beside her and filling the car with his over-whelming presence.

She felt the change in the vibrations around her as the car began to move away from the tangle of gridlock that surrounded the courthouse, but she couldn't force herself to open her eyes and look back. She felt like she'd run a marathon, but it had been less than five minutes since she'd stepped out of this limousine in front of the courthouse.

Her body shook and jerked in earnest now as the adrenaline coursed through her. Even her teeth chattered as she tried to inhale and exhale smoothly. It was useless, she knew this feeling far too well. She was headed for a full-scale panic attack and nothing would stop it. She leaned forward into the cloud of white silk and heard a pathetic whimper escape her lips as her breathing accelerated with brutal force.

She was vaguely aware of a sharp curse coming from nearby, but the sound was drowned out by the noise of her breath struggling to exit and enter her lungs.

When it came to comforting women, Eros would admit that most of his experience existed solely in the post-lovemaking glow of the bedroom. Comforting a woman he had just stolen away from her own wedding was another matter entirely.

She'd chosen to walk away on her own, he reminded himself. Perhaps if he repeated that to himself enough he might actually believe that his original plan hadn't begun to change from the moment he'd set eyes on Priya Davidson Khan in that hotel lobby. A new idea had begun to form, one that both excited him and filled him with unease.

He looked down at his stolen bride, her body swamped in his favourite tailored suit jacket and her ruined white gown and he felt something within him tighten uncomfortably. He'd come to New York intent on revenge. Intent on ruining his brother's precious public image and finally finding a way of dismantling the throne of corruption and lies his father had ruled for decades.

But then he'd laid eyes upon the woman he'd been sent to ruin and a wild idea had formed in his mind. A terrible, brilliant twist to his plan where he would not simply ruin his brother's chance at wedding his perfect bride.

He would steal her…for himself.

He was not in the habit of drawing innocent people into his plans and playing by the rules had never been his style but if a bride was what was required to fulfil the terms of the will fastest, he saw no better choice than the woman in front of him.

She was exactly the kind of bride his pompous, perfectionist brother would choose for this production he was putting on. The dutiful protégé, stepping into power with his society bride by his side. He probably planned to create an army of perfect little heirs to further lock up his hold over the empire he had no right to.

In planning his brother's ruination, he had dug into Priya's past enough to see that she had grown up in luxury, trained to move in only the most polished circles. Apart from an embarrassing engagement and messy break-up at eighteen, she was scandal-free. Perfect for an elitist fool like Xander.

But the past seven years of her life since her disastrous first failed jaunt down the aisle were strangely devoid of gossip, as though she'd ceased to exist. Now she had her face turned away from him as she calmed herself. Her hands were clasped in her lap, crushing a fistful of silk as though she wasn't sure if she wished to cry or throw a tantrum. Somehow, he didn't think she would allow herself to do either. She had quickly assumed a mask of complete control.

What would it take to unravel that glacial resolve?

Why was he so utterly fascinated by it?

He watched as she calmed herself down, using some kind of breathing exercise, and he decided that now was not the time to inform her about his original plan to have her photographed with him. He had dealt with the paparazzi and if they dared to defy him, they would regret it.

The world may think him a wild and reckless playboy but that was only because that was the image he presented to them. If Zeus had known the true power he possessed, how much wealth he had accumulated during the past fifteen years, he would have long ago turned his corrupt focus on him.

He had planned his careful takedown of the Mytikas empire for more than a decade, then, at the last hour, his bastard father had to go and die. Zeus had long ago chosen Xander, the oldest of his three by-blows, to be his sole heir. The idea that he would offer up the position to be easily snatched away by one of his rejected spares at the last moment was exactly the kind of power move Eros should have expected.

The car slowed down as they entered the sleek rows of residential towers that bordered the south end of Central Park. The driver manoeuvred them down a narrow alleyway to a discreet private entrance, partially hidden from the street.

Priya looked up as they came to a stop, her eyes glazed and unfocused. 'Where have you brought me?'

'Somewhere you can dry off and wait out the media storm.' He stepped out of the limousine and extended his hand to her, trying and failing not to notice the delicious display of skin on show as she struggled to gather the gown. It must weigh a significant amount, judging by the awkwardness of her movements.

Almost the moment the thought crossed his mind, he looked down to see her wrestling with the lower layer of silk, which had got stuck in the doorway.

'This is why I hate wearing dresses.' She punctuated the last word with a sharp pull, which quickly resulted in a loud ripping sound. She froze, wide-eyed and still completely trapped against the doorway.

Eros moved closer, surveying the gown. 'Allow me?'

After a moment she nodded and Eros leaned down, tearing the rest of the fabric free with one easy tug. But instead of stepping away, he pulled again, ripping the lower edge of the skirt from below her knees. The movement completely detached the heavy cloud of silk and netting from the underskirt, which still fitted snugly against her thighs. He stood back, surveying his work with a satisfied smirk.

'That was…completely unnecessary,' she said in horror.

'Forgive me, princess, were you planning on wearing it again?'

With a thoroughly unladylike growl, she stepped out of the larger mass of material and kicked the mud-splashed silk to one side.

'That's better.' He ensured his words were dry and disinterested as he avoided staring down at the perfect toned skin of her long legs.

Wide, molten chocolate eyes narrowed up at him with anger and Eros felt a flash of something suspiciously akin to enjoyment. No, he corrected the errant thought, attraction was what he felt. And why wouldn't he be attracted? She was a beautiful woman and he was a red-blooded male. He'd met plenty of beautiful women, but that didn't mean he had so little control as to act on it every time his libido roared to attention.

They remained in silence on the long ride up to his penthouse suite, for which Eros was grateful. The woman was a distraction and right now he needed to focus on his game plan. Once his mother realised what he was now planning to do…she would do everything within her power to put a stop to it. Time was not on his side…but maybe he could pull it off.

It all depended on whether or not he could convince the woman by his side that marriage was the most logical course of action for them both. A sentence he had never dared to think, let alone speak aloud.

The brand-new luxury tower was a pet project of his and comprised a series of condominiums with price tags that would make even the wealthiest magnate's eyes water. The lobby was a cavernous marble hall that dated back more than a century.

Antique mirrors and sumptuously dark fabric lined the hallway walls of his penthouse, accented by warm glowing sconces.

'I can't tell if this place is a restoration or brand new.' Her eyes widened as she stepped into the bright open-plan living space and gazed up at the bronze ceiling feature.

'It's one of my favourite things to do, to take a slice of history, preserve it and put it on show within something modern.' His architects had been given free rein to complete a building that was worthy of note in the history books. When he had seen the final plans, how the rest of the tower rose behind the original structure like a gleaming sword slicing into the sky, he'd been speechless.

He had never planned to live in Manhattan again, but he had taken the top-floor suite on impulse, having been bewitched by the warm stone floors, bronze details and the perfectly centred views over the park.

A strange chattering sound emanated from the woman beside him and he looked down to see her stubbornly trying to hide her discomfort as she stared around at the wide open-plan living space.

'It's b-beautiful.' She shivered.

Cursing under his breath, he decided to forgo a tour, taking her by the hand and guiding her into the spacious guest suite before ushering her into the bathroom.

'You're turning blue. That dress needs to come off.'

He heard Priya's swift intake of breath.

'I have nothing else to wear.'

'I have no wish to have you contract pneumonia under my watch, princess. You need a hot shower and dry clothing. Turn around.'

'Don't be ridiculous. I can manage.' She breathed shakily, staring down at the sodden gown with stubborn determination.

'I doubt you got into that dress alone.' He pointed to the layers of silk ribbons and loops, criss-crossing to hold the back of the gown together.

'You seem to know a lot about corsetry—are you a dressmaker?'

'I'll admit I have an appreciation for delicate lingerie. Mainly the act of removing it from a woman's body.' Eros didn't know whether to laugh or groan as he watched her absorb his words and unconsciously bite her lower lip.

'Okay, then,' she said, rather breathlessly. 'Try to be quick. I am quite cold.'

He was tempted to make another double entendre until she exhibited another racking shiver and he noticed her lips had taken on a dark tinge.

The dampness of the silk was a hindrance he hadn't foreseen, with each sharp pull only serving to slide the fabric a scant few centimetres. Cursing under his breath, he opened the drawer of the vanity and pulled out a small penknife. A few quick slides of the blade and the material began to sag open, revealing the smooth expanse of her bare back.

'Is it done?' She turned to look in the mirror, catching his eye as he slid his blade under the final loop.

'I'm afraid you won't be winning any fashion awards, but you can probably breathe again. How tight was that thing?'

'It's an object of torture.' She turned just as he moved outside the doorway, momentarily losing her grip on the dress so that it slid dangerously low on her chest.

Eros felt like the world moved in slow motion as inch by inch of creamy brown skin was revealed to his suddenly starving gaze. She was the perfect mix of softness and muscle, round in all the right places. She quickly covered herself back up to her chin.

'I should probably get warmed up too.' He watched her in the mirror and began to unbutton his shirt, noticing her eyes following the movement.

Her eyes widened and her tongue snaked out to moisten her bottom lip. As though realising he'd seen her reaction, she shook her head, slamming the bathroom door closed and turning the lock.

Dear God, if he didn't know better he would think she was a weapon sent to destroy his control. Women had always been his weakness, his preferred company and comfort. He had devoted his adult life to becoming a master of pleasure. Women seemed to seek him out for his supposed talents, then left in search of men they respected to settle down with, and that suited him just fine. But the last few months had been hectic with a slew of unexpected projects and he'd found he didn't have the usual time or energy to devote to seduction.

Then, the moment he'd arrived back in Athens and had been poised to revive an old acquaintance, his mother had arrived with her news.

He just needed to get laid, he told himself with a laugh as he disappeared into his own comfortable master suite, thankful for the brief reprieve from their sparring. He needed to regroup and reset his plans. He was a master of details but right now this all felt like an impulsive mess. He knew he was making the right move—he trusted his intuition, it had never steered him wrong—but what he didn't trust...was her.

Or was it that he didn't trust himself around her?

Hardly taking a moment to examine the space he'd spent an exorbitant amount of money on, he moved to the long floor-to-ceiling windows and gazed out into the distance. It had been such a long time since he'd set foot in this city that he'd almost forgotten about the breath-taking beauty that Manhattan had to offer.

He'd been raised in Greece but as a child of divorced parents he'd spent almost half of every year travelling with his jet-setting mother. Coming to prefer his mother's lax method of parenting over his stepfather's severe style, he'd spent much of his teenage and early twenties with New York and other major financial cities as his playground. Regret was a familiar pang against his breastbone as he let his eyes wander over the tall giants of steel and glass that formed the iconic skyline in the background and the lush green of the park spread out below.

He imagined what his stepfather would think, knowing Eros was about to do the one thing he'd warned him against. Though he had only been married to Arista for less than a decade, Stavros Theodorou had remained a constant presence in Eros's life and had given him more than any blood relative ever had. He was the man from whom he had taken his family name, the

man who had taught him to value loyalty above
all else.

Marriage is a trap, he would growl, his voice
pure gravel from years of chain smoking.

Unable to sit with his thoughts for another moment, Eros walked into the slate-walled bathroom and stripped, stepping under the harsh
spray of the waterfall shower.

A groan of pure pleasure escaped his throat
as the heat unravelled some of the knots in his
shoulders. The image of a certain pair of delicate hands, kneading his muscles, entered his
mind and he pushed the thought away with an
impatient frown.

His promises to his stepfather had driven him
for the past ten years. His regrets over how he
had treated the only person who had ever had
his best interests at heart still shamed him, but
he was determined to undo some of his wrongs.
Double-crossing Arista and teaching her a les-
son was the first step. Then, once he had inherited the majority shares of Mytikas Holdings he
would move his focus on to Xander.

Images of Priya bathing on the other side of
the wall entered his mind unbidden and he in-
dulged himself for a moment, imagining what it
might be like to unravel that polished stone exterior and reveal the molten heat he could sense
beneath.

CHAPTER THREE

PRIYA STARED AT her reflection in the floor-length mirror and wondered how on earth she had ended up in such a precarious position. She'd been so relieved to be free of the wedding gown she'd hardly even thought of what she would wear once she got out of the shower until a quick peek outside the bathroom door had revealed a freshly pressed white shirt laid out on the bed.

It was clearly excellent quality and expensive but it was designed to fit six feet plus of muscular Greek male, not her own meagre five and a half feet. The hem was respectable at least, covering her to just above her knee. And with few small adjustments, rolling up the sleeves and tucking in the collar…it almost passed for a chic dress.

Almost.

She walked back out into the open-plan living area and was relieved to find it empty. A polished wooden drinks bar took up one side of the dining area and she immediately busied herself, looking through the various vintage and luxury brands of whiskey. Selecting one she recognised as having been one of her father's favourites, she poured a glass and felt a familiar ache within as she inhaled the familiar scent. The sun had begun to set fast, setting the room ablaze with colour and drawing her gaze outside to the red and gold hues of the park far below.

Her body was tight with nerves as she felt the stillness of the cavernous apartment settle onto her like a dead weight. The amber liquid did nothing to ease the growing whirlpool of guilt and uncertainty swirling like acid in her gut.

'What have I done?' she whispered, hearing her heartbeat threatening to burst from her chest.

'You've recognised a poor investment and changed course.'

She turned, taking in the man who stood a few feet away and felt her stomach clench in response. His hair lay wet and curling upon his shoulders, only serving to accentuate the sharp cut of his cheekbones and that dangerous jawline. Gone was the three-piece suit, replaced now by a pair of form-fitting black jeans and a stone-grey sweater that looked luxuriously soft. He looked so effortlessly put together and here she stood in just a shirt, like a woman who had just fallen out of his bed. Of course he didn't even try to hide his perusal of her makeshift dress as he stalked towards her, closing the distance between them.

Priya stood her ground, despite the urge to run, or worse, to move closer. She couldn't have chosen a worse time to be struck down by something so inconvenient as an attraction. He eyed the glass in her hand, leaning forward until he was close enough to inhale the scent of the whiskey.

'You have excellent taste. This one is my favourite.' Their eyes met for a moment before he moved to pour himself a glass. He hummed low in his throat after the first taste and Priya felt a shiver run down her spine. Shaking off the uncomfortable sensation, she forced herself not to retreat as he focused on her once more.

'Come. We have things we need to discuss.' With effortless grace, he lowered his powerful frame onto a long leather sofa and gestured for her to take a seat by his side.

The move felt strangely intimate and Priya felt her brows rise in the face of such bald arrogance. Now that the adrenaline of the afternoon had begun to recede, anger bubbled just beneath the surface of her control. Taking another long sip of the vintage whiskey, she fought the urge to throw the liquid into his lap. 'I'd prefer to stand, thank you.'

'Suit yourself.' His fingers drummed a sharp rhythm on the arm of the chair.

'I'm not being ungrateful,' she said quickly, not quite able to look directly at him. Not unlike the blazing heat of a summer sun, Eros Theodorou was a risk to be approached with caution. The man exuded the kind of scorching male energy that she had always made a point of avoiding. But there was no avoiding her current situation and the fact that his vengeance-fuelled proposition was the only remaining chance she had to save her father's legacy.

The resentment left a bitter taste in her mouth. This was not a moment for pride, she reminded herself. There were people's livelihoods at stake.

With a single fortifying breath, she met the eyes of the man who was both tormentor and saviour. 'I'm very thankful for your assistance today, though I know your motives weren't exactly pure. Still… I've thought about it and I'd like to accept your offer.'

He was silent for a moment, his eyes focused on the amber liquid he swirled around in a glass on his knee. 'It's a pity…because that particular offer has now expired.'

Priya felt that single word reverberate in her mind with all the force of a thousand drums. *Expired.* 'Is that supposed to be a joke?'

'You walked away from me, Priya. You wounded my very fragile male pride.'

'There is nothing fragile about you or your ego,' she blurted, anger taking hold of her tongue. She took a single step towards where he sat, the injustice of it taking her breath away. 'Was this a part of your plan? You picked me up in front of all of those reporters…'

Something dark flickered in his eyes that looked suspiciously like guilt and Priya felt her insides drop with sudden realisation. '*You*. Of course, it was you who arranged for the paparazzi ambush. Now you've got exactly what you wanted without even paying a penny.'

'In my world, this is how business is done. I was not lying before, I would have paid your uncle's debts without any further action.'

'But now you have the upper hand.' She felt her lips twist with the realisation, cold fear sliding down her spine. 'Do you wish to make me beg for your help? Is that why you brought me here?'

She vaguely saw him place his glass on the floor and stand. The air felt too hot, the pressure in her chest growing by the second. This hadn't been a rescue; it had been an attack of conscience. He had no intention of helping her—why would he? She had refused his scandalous offer but then she'd still gone and jilted her groom. She'd been a pawn in someone else's game once again.

'I need to leave… I can't stay here.' She began walking towards the foyer and he was upon her in an instant, his big frame moving around her to block her path. He was close. So close that she could see a few rogue droplets of water slide from his slicked-back hair and down his neck. The drops disappeared down into the vee of his sweater and she felt herself swallow convulsively past the dryness in her throat.

'You will not run from me, Priya,' he grated out, something wild and untameable glowing in his eyes.

'Why would I stay here a moment longer? So you can threaten to send scandalous pictures to the press and ruin me even further?' she challenged, pushing past him but having her progress hampered by the obstruction of one very large, very muscular male hand against the wall beside her head.

'The reporters were there purely to anger my brother and further the scandal. Once they'd chased you I called them off. As it stands, there will be no mention of your connection to me in the press. But if you go running from my building wearing only one of my shirts… There is only so much damage control I can do.' There was no amusement in his tone now, only thinly veiled anger that made her skin prickle with awareness. Her breath came in sharp bursts, his proximity not helping matters. Almost as though he'd heard her thoughts, he released her from the cage of his arms and put some space between them.

'Surely the whole point of it was to have them target me, as well.' Priya closed her eyes. 'You tricked me into that limo, knowing exactly what you planned to do.'

A muscle ticked in his jaw. 'Originally, yes.'

She felt despair settle upon her like a dead weight, making her shoulders slump back against the wall as her heart continued to pound against her ribs. She felt like she had entered a fever dream where nothing made sense. She needed to leave and get back to the tiny apartment she'd rented in the East Village and try to find a way to regroup.

'I'm handling this poorly.' Eros spoke from a few steps away.

'You think?' She forced her eyes away from him, feeling her pulse pound uncomfortably at his proximity. Her awareness of his blatant male energy was just another source of irritation to her overloaded mind.

Eros mimicked her posture, leaning one broad shoulder against the opposite wall. But while she imagined that she looked fragile and exhausted, he looked fresh and virile, a man who knew he held all the power. God, what she would give to shift that balance back where it belonged. To take control of her own destiny once and for all.

'I don't want to make you beg, Priya. You're far too valuable for those kinds of games. I want to offer you an alternative,' Eros said. 'A way that we can both get what we want.'

'You're quite optimistic that I'd believe you.'

His words held no amusement now as he watched her, his full lips pressed in a hard line. 'You are probably aware of the stipulations of the last will and testament left by my dear father?'

She didn't answer his assumption, allowing him to continue.

'You see, I find myself in a similar legal situation to my dear brother. One that also requires the immediate acquisition of a bride.'

Priya felt the shock of his words hit her in the chest. Had she heard him correctly? Was this why Xander had been so adamant on rushing their wedding?

'Are you suggesting that I fill that position?' she asked.

'Suggesting…advising…' He made a rough gesture with his hands, his posture relaxed. 'Marriage to me would be infinitely more entertaining, don't you think?'

'Why would I marry you?' The words burst from her lips unbidden.

'It's the perfect solution. We are both equally bound by the need for a hasty wedding.'

'I can't imagine you being bound by anything.' She saw a glimmer in his gaze and immediately regretted the picture her own words evoked. Clearing her throat, she shook off the image, hardly believing she was entertaining this offer at all. 'Why on earth would I trust you?'

'Because a man in my position can provide the financial backing and influence you need to force your uncle to do exactly as you ask. I can clear his debts and relieve him of his shares in the process while also ensuring the information is kept confidential. I have powerful lawyers in my employ who would be at your disposal. After one year, once we have both achieved our separate goals, we would part ways.'

'You honestly think it's that simple?' she asked, wondering why she was even listening to another offer from a man who'd already proved himself to be untrustworthy.

'Anyone in your situation would jump at the chance.'

'You admitted to seeking revenge on my fiancé today, hardly a great basis for a new partnership of any kind.'

He took a step closer, not quite crowding her

but still setting her nerves further on edge. 'My paragon of a brother is no longer your fiancé.' His voice was a low purr. 'I'll admit that I am largely motivated by revenge on your former groom. I have made no secret that I pride myself on winning, Priya.'

'I am not a competition to be won,' she snapped, awed by his sheer audacity.

He had been raised to believe he was a god, no doubt, and so was utterly unable to perceive the idea that a mere female like her might not want him. 'I know my worth. I know that by marrying me you would have access to my fortune to do with as you wish and, quite frankly, from what I know of you… I cannot take that risk.'

'I have no need for your money or your father's firm and its history of dwindling assets. Accept my terms and I will have a prenuptial agreement drawn up tonight and signed by morning. It would be a private agreement. No theatrics, no publicity of any kind.'

'A prenuptial…' She frowned, her thoughts becoming scattered as she fought to process the possibility in his words. 'This is insane.'

'You say you know your worth, well, there we are well matched. I am willing to offer you a short-term, equal partnership whereby you can turn the tables on your uncle and take control of your fortune yourself. Alone.'

Priya froze, hardly believing what he was saying. She'd always planned to take it slowly and earn her place at Davidson Khan. Was she ready for that kind of power? She'd only graduated with her master's degree four years ago but her reputation as a talented mind in the financial world was already well known from her time working for major firms in London and Dubai.

'Marriage to me would be a business contract, Priya. I have no need for a society bride and I suspect you would not enjoy the public scrutiny of jilting one groom for another while you attempt to take the helm of Davidson Khan. There would be a gag order in place to protect both of our interests, but I would need to take measures one step further. If you agree to become my bride, we leave New York and you can't return or have any contact with the outside world until I allow it.'

Priya blinked, her brain struggling to process all the information. 'Are you actually proposing to lock me away until you decide when I will be released? Like I'm some kind of prisoner?'

'It would only be for a few weeks at most, but there would be no actual chains involved...unless you're into that kind of thing?' He raised a brow in her direction, his lips quirking.

'Be serious.' She straightened her shoulders, ignoring the image his words conjured up. 'What exactly would I be expected to do for that length of time? Where would you take me?'

'That I can't reveal either. Not until you've signed a prenup.'

'You expect me to blindly agree to your outrageous terms and yet you don't trust me with your own plans?'

'I have never offered you my trust, Priya. Neither do I expect any from you. It's human nature for people to hold their own best interests at heart.'

'That almost passed for philosophical.'

'I'm full of surprises.' He smirked, extending his hand to her. 'So, do you agree to my terms?'

She hesitated for a long moment, mulling over his words. Could she really allow herself to be whisked away to some unknown location, like a stolen prize? She thought of her uncle's face and the rage he'd no doubt flown into once he'd realised she was running from the wedding. If she didn't stop him, he'd destroy everything her father had worked so hard for. He would destroy the legacy that was always meant to be hers.

Suddenly, a dangerous thought occurred to her.

She didn't have to trust Eros Theodorou to accept his offer. She could use him, just as she'd been used so many times in the past. She could accept his offer and use his wealth and power as a stepping stone. Even his ridiculous terms could serve as a valuable period to feign her own defeat while she regrouped and formulated her plans. She didn't need to know where he was taking her, only that it was far away from Manhattan. Then, once the time was right, she would return and lay claim to everything that was rightfully hers.

'Okay, I'll do it. I'll marry you.' She heard the words escape her lips on a breath while her heart pounded. 'What happens next?'

Eros's expression was filled with a dark glimmer of triumph as his gaze lowered to take in the glittering diamond she still wore on her left hand. 'You can start by taking his ring off.'

She looked down, flexing her fingers in the low light. She'd almost forgotten about the delicate princess-cut diamond that had been delivered to her home days before the wedding along with a bouquet of beautiful yellow roses. There had been no note, nothing to make it seem more than the simple business arrangement she'd agreed to. But the idea of wearing Xander's ring had filled her with such anxiety she'd left it in the box, only sliding it onto her finger for the handful of public appearances they'd made in the week before. Being seen with her on his arm had been very important to her former groom.

'I'd planned on returning it.' Priya toyed with

the platinum band, not quite liking the tone in Eros's voice, or the idea of being commanded to remove the ring as though it were a symbol of ownership. She was not passing from one man's hands to the next. She was a smart business-woman with autonomy who had decided to swap a poor deal for one with less risk.

The thought that perhaps her formerly intended groom may not have known the extent of Uncle Vikram's duplicity made her pause. But the damage had already been done. She twirled the ring around and around, feeling the guilt she'd been suppressing finally rise to greet her. 'I feel like perhaps he is owed an explanation.'

'Give me your hand.' His voice was like a sharp whip in the silence, snapping her focus back to him. His features hard and unyielding, he stepped forward and extended his hand to her. She surprised herself by following his order, placing her left hand in his before she had the good sense to question herself. With surprising softness, he opened her palm out slowly and slid the ring from her third finger with one smooth movement. The sensation made her shiver invol-untarily…or was it the intensity in his eyes as he pocketed the small piece of metal and rubbed once over the bare skin left behind?

A long silence spread out between them and Priya found herself completely unable to look up, needing a moment to gather her thoughts without the intensity she knew she would find in his gaze. He seemed to do everything with such purpose, such bold confidence, she couldn't help but feel a bit steamrollered with every new interaction. And yet he gave her the space to make her choice with almost infuriating consistency. She might tell herself she'd been backed into a corner but the reality was it had been she who had done it. If anything, he'd offered her a way to get out with her dignity intact.

The memory of running from the crowd of onlookers in her giant gown was still fresh. As was every moment leading up to her scandalous exit. Feeling all those eyes upon her, judging her...

A stern voice jolted her from her thoughts. 'Look at me.'

She looked up and was met with barely restrained fury blazing behind the blue depths of his gaze.

'You owe him nothing, *me akous*.' His voice seemed to deepen, slipping into what she presumed to be his native Greek. He shook his head once, catching himself. 'Do you understand me, Priya?'

She hesitated, chewing on her lower lip as she fought against the urge to simply agree. He was effortlessly authoritative with his impressive height and stern brooding glare. But she had never been the kind of woman to sit back and submit to anyone's orders, especially not those of a man she had only just met.

Shaking off the spell he seemed to have put her under, she moved away from him, seeking the airy freedom of the balcony as she tried to conceal the tremor of anxiety that threatened to overtake her composure.

Eros fought not to smile as Priya silently seethed with rage in the wake of his commands. He knew he had been pushing too far by issuing an outright order but hearing her talk of owing Xander anything had lit a fire of anger within him. His brother was a calculating bastard, and he had no doubt the other man knew exactly what he'd been doing when he'd accepted the deal with his fiancée's uncle without her explicit consent.

'Why do I get the impression that you are far more trouble than I anticipated?' he mused.

'Because I prefer to know my own mind rather than nod and go along with every testosterone-charged request you make of me?' she responded. 'If I had known that by accepting your help I was entering into some kind of tug of war between you and—'

'You know nothing about the situation.'

'Seeing as I've just agreed to marry you, perhaps you could enlighten me?'

Eros felt familiar anger seethe and roil just beneath the surface of his control. He had long ago learned that anger was just as vulnerable to manipulation as love or trust. Anger was far more unpredictable and far more easily incited. He looked down at the woman before him, this beautiful lamb who had unknowingly stepped into the middle of a battlefield. She may be innocent in all of this, but that did not make her his ally.

Less than a few hours ago she had been set to become the bride of his enemy. He had seen the play of emotions over her face, the guilt, the care. She had no idea of the truth of the man she'd been about to wed. She had no idea the truth behind their family name, the lies and the greed.

The legacy of Zeus was so potent he had ensured he caused chaos even after his death. Of the three sons he'd sired, Xander Mytikas was the most like their father. Cruel, calculating and obsessed with his precious image.

'I wasn't prepared to sacrifice my humanity in the quest for my father's approval. Let's just say that my brother made a very different choice. He chose the prospect of power over the chance to do the right thing. Just as he planned to do with you.'

Fury pulsed within him, pushing against his control. Tightening his fists, he forced a smile to his lips and sighed with practised nonchalance, forcing himself to look away from the beguiling effect of the sunshine reflecting in the deep amber of her eyes.

'Marriage may be a binding legal agreement, but there is nothing in the vows to influence morality.'

'Is that your way of telling me not to trust you either, Eros?'

Hearing his name on her lips for the first time distracted him momentarily and he found himself looking back once more, getting drawn into the steady, serious force of her gaze. She didn't look away, remaining utterly still as she assessed him. When had a woman ever looked at him this way? As though she was trying to unravel the outer shell he presented to the world in order to see beneath. For a man who prided himself on using his charm to control every interaction, it was…uncomfortable.

'Blind, open trust is a myth. Without incentive or consequences, people will always act in their own best interests. I plan to apply both to our situation effectively.'

'You're talking about a prenup?'

He nodded once. 'I have spent a decade building my own empire on my own terms, free from the corruption and sacrifice required under the rotting logo of Mytikas Holdings. I may be many terrible, scandalous things…but in business I protect my own. Once we're married, like it or not, you fall under that term.'

'So, as your wife, I'd be on par with your employees? I'm honoured.'

'It's a hazardous position.' He leaned against the stone balustrade. 'Many women have tried and failed to get my ring on their finger. The backlash may become dangerous.'

His words earned the tiniest flicker of humour on her full lips, and he forced himself to look away. 'I received word that your friend has been causing quite a stir, attempting to hunt you down.'

She stood up straight. 'Aria? I should speak with her.'

Eros met her eyes with silent warning. 'You remember our bargain? No one can know about our deal until I choose it.'

She folded her arms across her chest and her eyes darkened with anger but she managed to keep the same coolness to her voice. 'You can't plan to lock me away immediately? I have things I need to get from my apartment, my clothes and my planner. I have a life too, Eros. I need to tell my friend that I'm okay.'

Eros considered her words for a moment, then slid his phone from his pocket and placed it in her palm. 'You have three minutes.'

After instructing her to keep the call on loud-speaker, Eros kept his eyes on Priya as she paced the foyer with her back turned to him.

The call was answered after barely one ring and a woman's voice filled the room. Priya winced as her friend immediately began berating her for disappearing.

'Relax. I'm fine, I'm safe.' She took a quick look over her shoulder. 'I found another way to solve my problem but I need to leave town for a few weeks.'

'Another way? Another groom, you mean?' the woman asked. 'Where are you going? Where is he taking you?'

Priya's voice flattened. 'Look, it's complicated and I can't go into it for legal reasons...but Vikram lied. This is the only way I can still save the company.'

Her friend was quiet for a long moment and he noticed Priya looked down at the screen to make sure the call hadn't been disconnected. 'You still there?'

Her friend's voice was filled with emotion. 'I don't like this. I don't like any of it.'

'I don't like it either, but it's what I need to do.'

Eros felt something dark rise within him at her words. He tapped the dial of his watch with pointed impatience, seeing her eyes narrow in response. She spoke quickly into the phone. 'Look, it will all be fine. I'll explain everything once I'm back.'

The other woman's voice lowered slightly. 'If you can't talk, just say yes or no. I heard Xander send guards in pursuit of his brother…there was this really intense, dark-haired man with a European accent. Italian, I think. Are you with him?'

Eros moved quickly, capturing Priya's hands and ending the call with one touch to the screen.

'That was rude.' She levelled an angry gaze at him, dark brown eyes filled with fury, and tried to pull her hands free from his grip.

'You were going to answer her question.'

'I don't break my word,' she gritted. 'But who was she talking about? Who did Xander see if it wasn't you?'

Eros thought for a moment, a wry smile pricking at one corner of his lips. 'I suspect that perhaps I am not the only of Zeus's bastard sons who came to break up your wedding. A fact that may work in my favour.'

'There are more of you?' Priya's eyes widened.

'It's not our concern. From now on, you will have no contact with your friend or anyone else until I allow it. This may not be a traditional marriage but I do not tolerate disloyalty in any form.' He looked down at his phone screen, seeing messages that had come in from the team of lawyers he'd kept on standby for the night. He had many things that needed to be done if he was going to pull this off. Many separate pieces to juggle before he staged his quiet retreat to Greece.

His retreat…with his stolen bride.

His eyes seemed to gravitate to the smooth skin of her long legs of their own accord, drinking in the beauty of her shape before finally reaching her face. She was the picture of quiet fury and he could understand why.

A woman of her intelligence and accomplishments being bound by such an archaic inheritance clause was akin to caging a wild tiger and expecting it to play the docile house pet. Her uncle deserved to lose everything and he would take pleasure in meting out the first step of that punishment.

He was slightly uneasy about the seeming calm she'd shown since accepting his offer. He wasn't as vain as to think she would be jumping for joy but he'd at least expected a little resistance.

Realising he was late to the emergency meeting he'd called with his legal team, he pulled on the leather jacket he'd slung over a nearby chair and took a moment to slick back his still-damp hair in the mirror. In the reflection, he saw Priya watching him.

'You're leaving?' She spoke with feigned nonchalance but he saw the small furrow that appeared between her brows. 'You expect me to just wait around this apartment alone until the ceremony?'

'I will need to move fast if we hope to be married by tomorrow night.' He pressed the button for the ground floor, using fingerprint technology, and leaned against the open doorway of the elevator.

'Tomorrow night?' He heard the shock in her voice. 'How is that even possible?'

'I make it my business to achieve the impossible. In this instance, however, it's nothing so miraculous, just a simple waiver and the right connections.' He took in the tightness of her features and almost laughed. Most of his past entanglements would have been overjoyed at the prospect of nabbing him as a husband but this woman looked like she might bolt at any moment.

'This building is security-protected. I will know if you attempt to break our terms and I do not appreciate being double-crossed.'

'I'm the one who usually gets taken for a fool so I could say the same to you.'

He chuckled to himself, taking a step back and pushing the button for the ground floor. 'I will have your things collected and couriered here. In the meantime, princess, get some rest.'

CHAPTER FOUR

WHEN PRIYA STEPPED out of the shower the next morning, she found her luggage had been delivered and placed just inside her bedroom door. Still dressed only in her towel, she dug out her trusty planner and sat down to write a quick entry, crossing off the date before marked 'Wedding' and adding a new one. She knew it was strange, how she needed something as silly as a planner, but it worked. She had long ago learned to embrace anything that quietened the hum of her own mind.

Her father had always called her a worrier, while her mother had proclaimed her only child to be self-centred and highly strung. She now knew that anxiety was simply something she managed. But the night before, in the darkness of Eros's guest bedroom, without a cell phone or laptop to busy herself with, she had been forced to endure the hum of her own mind and its attempts to grasp the unexpected turn her life had taken.

As a result, her eyes now burned from the scant few hours she'd managed to sleep and her shoulders were so tense they ached. But she was fine, she told herself sternly as she focused on dressing in her favourite skinny jeans and a soft woollen sweater. The apartment was silent as she padded barefoot out of her room in search of food. She hadn't eaten a thing since lunch the day before and now her body was in full rebellion. Feeling a little shaky, she opened the fridge and grabbed the first thing she saw, a large platter of perfectly sliced cantaloupe. Without a second thought, she bit into the first piece and groaned with relief as the sweetness hit her tongue.

The sudden clearing of a throat directly behind her almost made her choke. She turned, expecting to see a particularly irritating Greek smirk, but instead was greeted by the sight of a tall grey-haired man, flanked by a younger man and woman who calmly revealed that they were there to finalise the prenuptial agreement.

The prospect of doing anything remotely resembling work made her synapses light up with glee and she spent the next hour reading the agreement and questioning and ensuring there were no loopholes in it. Once Eros had discreetly paid her uncle's debts and purchased the majority shares, he would be legally obliged to transfer them directly into Priya's name. As they finished the process, a phone call was made and the grey-haired man began speaking in what sounded like rapid Greek. After a moment he extended the phone towards her. 'He would like to speak to you.'

Priya stood, moving quickly out onto the balcony for privacy.

'Everything is to your satisfaction?' a familiar accented voice rumbled on the other end of the line.

'I've agreed to all of your terms, and I'm officially bound by the law not to reveal your evil plans.' She shivered in the cool air, wrapping her arm around herself. 'The lawyers mentioned that I will need my passport. I'd like to know where I'm being taken once we are married.'

'Patience, Priya.' His voice was playful but underlined with steel. 'I've left a gift for you in the foyer. I'll see you at six.'

The line went dead and Priya fought the urge to curse aloud in the most unladylike fashion. She was irritated by his obvious mistrust, but reminded herself that he had warned her that she would be kept in the dark. It was fine, she told herself as she escorted the lawyers to the elevator, smiling tightly until she was once again left alone. There was no reason to worry.

She hadn't even officially begun working at Davidson Khan, yet they had an excellent structural team already in place. Once the shares had been transferred, there was no reason the company wouldn't just continue to run as normal.

It would be just like taking a vacation. She closed her eyes and stretched the tense muscles in her shoulders. Of course, she hated vacations, but she would deal with the boredom by planning her strategy for stepping into her new role. Judging by the amount of time her new fiancé had chosen to spend with her so far, she would most likely be left to her own devices, which suited her just fine.

Her thoughts consumed by the future, she almost missed the large parcel that had been left on the side table. The packaging was expensive and marked with the name of one of her favourite Fifth Avenue boutiques. A sleek black card bearing a golden archer logo lay on top:

Don't rip this one.
E

She frowned as she took the box into the bedroom and opened it up, pulling away layers of tissue paper. Inside she found a pair of butter-soft ivory silk tailored trousers and a matching fitted blazer. The sizing was perfect and she wondered if he had guessed just by looking at her or if he'd had someone go digging for that information. Pushing that uncomfortable thought away, she looked through the rest of the packages and found a detailed ivory corset and matching thong.

Of course he would buy her lingerie. Still, the corset was clearly designed to show at the apex of the blazer to soften the look. It was a pity she couldn't wear it. Wearing this suit would be a show of submission and the balance of control was already sliding uncomfortably beyond her reach.

More than likely he hadn't even chosen it himself, she told herself as she undressed and quickly showered, deliberately leaving the package out of her eyeline. She didn't really have anything appropriate of her own, other than one of her plain black work suits, but maybe keeping this professional was a good course of action. Yes, that was a good plan.

Throughout her short, sparse dating history she had been given compliments on her dark eyes and curvaceous body, but she had never been called a great beauty. Her Indian heritage and serious expression had always made her easily recognisable next to the rows of smiling blonde heiresses at society balls and she'd got some attention, but she'd never cared much about what she wore or how she looked.

Eros had openly assessed her attributes and what she had seen in his gaze led her to believe that he found her physically appealing but he had not objectified her in the way she would have expected from a man with his reputation.

She may or may not have lain awake until dawn, agonising over her decision and searching her mind for information on the man she'd just agreed to marry. Would she be foolish for believing the media narrative without asking the man himself? Even as the thought entered her head she brushed it away. One could not possibly fabricate a reputation of wild nights out and strings of affairs with beautiful women.

As her father had often told her, if it walked and talked like a duck, it was a duck. As uncomfortable as it made her feel to tie her name to a man like him, the worst thing she could possibly do was start imagining that perhaps he wasn't what he said he was.

She took some time fixing her hair into a sleek chignon at the base of her head, finishing it off with a delicate gold slide that was encrusted in tiny pearls and diamonds. The piece had belonged to her great-grandmother and had been brought to the United States from Mumbai almost eighty years previously. She still remembered the look of pride in her father's eyes when he had presented it to her at her first debutante ball.

It had been traditionally worn by brides in their family and although the wealthy Khan family had since joined their name with the elite Davidsons and become steadily less bound by the traditions of their ancestors as each generation passed, this one had somehow stuck. After her first disaster of an engagement she had put the piece away, never believing she would wear it again. She still didn't know quite how she had allowed herself to be pushed into such an agreement. But sometimes that was how it worked, wasn't it? You believed that you were still in control but the control had been taken from you so slowly you didn't notice until it was too late.

Eros had casually mentioned her first attempt at matrimony, not knowing how powerful a weapon he had wielded. That dark moment in her history had shaped everything that she was and had been the catalyst for her walk away from the sizeable inheritance that had been hers. It had forced her to discover who she was without her father's wealth and had made her the woman she was now.

The decision to step back into this world and manipulate the stipulations in her father's will had not been taken lightly. She had thought she'd found the best solution to save her father's legacy and keep her fortune out of her mother's and her uncle's hands. Eros had been an unwitting angel in disguise, really. Even though she was not maintaining full control of her fortune, she knew that she would never allow herself to be controlled or manipulated in that way again.

She had just finished applying some basic make-up when the intercom buzzed, heralding the arrival of a driver to take her to the ceremony. Evidently, Eros was not planning to see her until they were face to face at whatever altar or judge's desk he had commandeered this late on a Monday evening.

Her plain black trousers and blazer lay flat on her bed, ready for her to make a statement of her own, but she couldn't stop her eyes from gravitating once again towards the garment box she'd pushed to the side.

What exactly would a secret wedding to Greece's most scandalous playboy entail? Perhaps a show of faith and compliance might suit her better than such an early rebellion. She needed to keep him on her side if he was to rescue her company from ruin after all. Before she could rethink it, she grabbed the box and pulled out its lavish contents once more.

The silk slid over her fingers as she quickly dressed and stepped in front of the floor-length mirror in the corner of the room. For several minutes the only sound was her own shallow breathing as she stared at her reflection.

She looked at herself from all angles, awed at how the lines transformed her into something very soft and feminine while still maintaining its power-suit appeal. She almost wished she had hated it, just so she didn't give him the satisfaction of admitting how perfect his selection had been.

The intercom buzzed once more, jolting her from the moment and forcing her into action. Her stomach flipped over as she took a deep breath and stepped into the elevator. There was no turning back now.

Eros told himself that having the quick ceremony at sunset in Central Park was functional and easier to contain on short notice than booking a venue or walking into City Hall. The semi-darkness and leafy foliage provided cover, as did the handful of guards he had ordered to block off the pathway to the pavilion and the judge who had agreed to marry them under special licence.

The delicate light green and grey iron structure known as the Ladies Pavilion sat nestled in between the trees and the rocky descent to the water, providing a spectacular view of the lake and the skyline beyond. This wedding may be a business deal but she had already run from two grooms, and he had no interest in becoming the third. So he had taken a calculated risk, sending her the ivory suit as a gift and allowing her the freedom of walking herself down the aisle. Or rather the dirt path, in this case.

He frowned down at the muddy edges of the path and hoped that she didn't have an aversion to nature. He had chosen neutral ground, an open space where they were not trapped, and this place had been the first one to come to mind.

As he looked out at the sun over the skyline reflected in the still surface of the lake, he listened to the sound of the city just beyond the trees. There was nothing peaceful about Manhattan, but this small corner of the park was probably the closest to solitude that one could get.

There had once been a time when this city had been his playground, with his older brother at his side and the world at their feet.

But there was no risk of his older brother coming to play his best man. Not now when Eros had stolen Xander's perfect bride for his own.

'Your paperwork is in order and we are ready to go. Are you sure she is on her way?' the elderly judge asked. Her husband had accompanied her, standing silently in the background, prepared to act as witness.

'She'll be here.' He gave her his most charis-

matic smile, trying not to look back towards the
lamp-lit path. He was not worried about Priya
running from *this* wedding, he reminded himself.
He had made sure that she had nothing to run
from, but he had also made it impossible for her
to disappear without his knowledge. He had assigned a skilled bodyguard to escort her for her
own safety as well as his. If she had decided to
go back on their deal, he would know.

His temples throbbed from a night of little
sleep. Along with the task of keeping tabs on
both of his brothers, his company, Arcum Investments, had just leased brand-new premises
in New York and with an impromptu honeymoon
planned, he had many loose ends to tie up before he disappeared with Priya. He had also had
his team put on the case of acquiring Davidson
Khan and clearing its CEO of his rather sizeable debts. Just like with every other investment
they undertook, Arcum would need to make sure
all the paperwork was airtight before they made
their final move.

Just as he began to feel tension build within
him, the judge gasped softly beside him. Eros
turned to follow her gaze and saw an ethereal
vision in white appear at the end of the lamp-
lit path.

She was all long legs and high heels, gliding
towards him with her piercing dark gaze and full

pursed lips. Yesterday, when she had stepped out of the elevator in her haute couture wedding gown, he had been struck by the sadness in her expression in the moments before she'd seen him and put her shields up. She'd seemed smaller, somehow. Like the force within her had been quietened. She had been obviously out of her comfort zone in the wedding gown and now he could see the difference with his own eyes.

In this bridal outfit, she didn't just walk, she strutted. She stood tall, the ivory silk seeming to hug every curve and dip of her body as she walked towards him. The pearls and beading on the undergarment that covered her chest seemed to glitter like diamonds as she passed under the golden glow of the lamps.

He saw the briefest bit of confusion and surprise on her face as she took in the setting he'd chosen but she shut it down quickly, adopting a serene expression as she navigated the steps in her heels. Bright red heels that seemed to be a perfect match for the intricate little ornament she wore in her hair.

He didn't know why but it gave him a small flare of pleasure that she had dressed for the occasion even though they both knew that this was not a true wedding. He allowed himself the briefest moment to take her in, noting her face was free of the elaborate make-up that had adorned her the day before, and her hair was a simple sleek style. He got the feeling that this was her true preference…simplicity.

Was it possible that she truly did not care about the wealth she had inherited?

Perhaps they were not so different after all. She intrigued him with her unreadable expression and fierce passion for what she cared for. Perhaps this short time they would be forced to stay together would not be quite unbearable.

The judge quickly moved forward to greet her, shaking her hand and guiding her towards the spot where Eros stood still and watching.

'You're late,' he heard himself say.

'It's customary for the bride to make her groom wait.' A small smile graced her lips but he saw the subtle flare of irritation in her eyes.

Eros smiled and felt himself relax for the first time in hours as they both turned and listened to the words that the judge began to say, reaffirming their prenuptial agreement.

Their vows were short and to the point, but still contained the usual promises to love and honour. When the moment finally came to slide the ring onto his bride's finger, he was surprised to feel his throat contract around the words, stopping him.

He had sworn he would never do this. That he would never make these kinds of impossible promises to another human being. Promises of the loving kind were just asking for disappointment and heartbreak. He'd had enough of both to last him a lifetime. Inhaling a deep breath, he forced himself to refocus and concentrate on the goal at hand. To remind himself that there were no hearts on the table and therefore no risk in that regard.

He took the smaller of the two gold bands and slowly slid the ring onto Priya's finger. Despite the placid, disinterested expression on her face, he felt her fingers tremble beneath his own. When it was her turn to place the larger ring on his finger, claiming him as her husband and vowing to honour him, he found he was unable to look away.

The rest of the ceremony passed in a haze of signatures as the judge ensured everything was above board. Priya kept her gaze downward but swore she could feel Eros watching her. He could have chosen anywhere for this part of their arrangement. They could have worn sweatpants to City Hall and it wouldn't have made a difference. Unless... A thought occurred to her just as a gentle flash illuminated them in the cocoon of lamplight they'd been under.

Priya looked behind them and, sure enough, a single photographer stood at the steps of the pavilion. Her eyes flew to Eros, but his expression was unreadable. The guards did not move to stop the photographer, which meant…he had been invited.

He had said they needed to make this look real in order for it to be accepted as a true marriage. But every second of the ceremony made something within her ache.

The judge had been speaking, she realised with a jolt, pulling her attention back to the very real moment she was living.

'I now pronounce you husband and wife,' the older woman declared, a wide smile lighting up her face as she took a step back. 'You may now kiss the bride.'

Priya felt every muscle in her body tighten in response to such a simple, common sentence. She was wearing white, he had put a ring on her finger. A kiss was the natural next step. And yet their agreement had seemed so theoretical until now. Suddenly everything seemed very, very real.

'We don't need to,' she said quickly, already feeling far too warm from the heat of the strong hands that still held hers. 'I mean…it's not necessary.'

The judge frowned and Priya immediately cursed herself for her own sharp tongue.

'She is nervous,' Eros purred in that low tone

she'd now come to recognise as one of intense enjoyment of her discomfort. 'I'd love nothing more right now than to kiss my beautiful bride.'

Priya forced a serene smile on her face as she took one bold step forward. She was not a coward. One meaningless kiss would not jeopardise their arrangement. She told herself that she was still in control...until Eros took a step forward to seal the space between them. She felt the air whoosh from her lungs as one powerful arm wrapped around her waist, holding her much too close. Not close enough, that dark voice within her protested. Inhaling on a gasp, she forced herself to look up, to meet the heat of his gaze as he dipped his head towards hers in what felt like slow motion.

At the same moment his lips touched hers, his other hand reached up to cup the side of her neck with a firm sensuality that felt far too heated for a judge's gaze. His skin seemed to set her aflame with that touch, holding her in place as he gently increased the pressure of his mouth on hers. Even without words, she felt like he was goading her, trying to get a reaction. She tried to remain dispassionate, telling herself that she wouldn't give in to such a blatant challenge. But her body didn't seem to get the memo in that regard.

He was simply proving his point about attraction, she told herself. But, still, her body was crying out to deepen the kiss… She tightened her hands into fists to resist the insane urge to wind her fingers into his hair.

He was the enemy, she reminded herself. He had taken charge of her destiny and intertwined it with his own.

The tiniest touch of his tongue against her lips made her body shiver, involuntarily pressing against him. The strong heat of his hand flexed hard on her hip and the delicious pressure sent pulses of electricity down every nerve ending. Suddenly she could no longer resist. She opened to him, all rational thought leaving her as she gloried in the scent of him, the heat of their kiss. She slid her own tongue against his and thought she heard a low growl coming from deep in his throat.

A faint cough came from nearby, along with the sound of the judge's amused chuckle, and just like that, it was as if a spell had been broken. Priya froze, realising how completely she had been swept away. Eros immediately released her from the shockingly sensual clinch they'd fallen into. She could still feel the heat of his hand on her neck…on her hip…

Had she *moaned*?

'Now I see why you were in such a rush to wed.' The judge smiled and shook their hands, walking them to the edge of the pavilion before wishing them a long and prosperous future together.

Priya's heart hammered in her chest as she studiously avoided looking at the man by her side while she tried to get a firm handle on her runaway libido.

That had not been how this was supposed to go.

She'd spent the past seven years of her life completely unaffected by the handsome, powerful men she'd encountered daily. They'd barely been married two minutes and she was already letting down her boundaries? What on earth had got into her? Like a wild dream, the past couple of minutes replayed in her mind and she fought not to turn away and hide her discomfort at her own loss of control. Instead, she met his gaze head on. Daring him to say something. To her surprise, his face was utterly devoid of expression.

They walked in silence through the park, flanked by a trio of discreet bodyguards to where a limo waited for them.

'Are the guards really necessary?' she asked, needing to redirect the subject as he slid into the dark interior of the car beside her, bringing with him the subtle scent of spice and sandalwood.

'In marrying me, my enemies are now yours.' He closed the door with a sharp thud, turning to face her. 'Let's just say that you are a very valuable investment.'

'And the photographs? Are they for my protection too?' She tried to remain calm but her heart still skittered uncomfortably in her chest from his kisses and she felt totally off balance. She hated feeling off balance. 'Eros, you might not care for your reputation but if I am going to be taking the helm of Davidson Khan I need to care about mine.'

'The photographs are to assure the legitimacy of our marriage can't be contested. They will not appear in the media. I told you, this arrangement remains between us until I choose to reveal it.'

'In going into hiding, do we not appear weak?'

'Patience, Priya. There is a difference between hiding in fear and controlling the narrative as one prepares for a full-scale attack.'

She thought on his words for a moment, then realisation dawned. 'You plan to make a play for control of Mytikas? But…how?'

'What better way to destroy a kingdom than from the throne itself?' He sat back lazily in the seat, watching her from beneath hooded lids. 'Don't worry, I don't plan to change the terms of our agreement. You will not be required to play the role of my wife in public over the next year. Unlike your former fiancé, I have no need to foster a good reputation.'

She exhaled a hard breath, still not able to shake the knots in her stomach. The lights of Manhattan passed by in a blur and she realised that they were not going back in the direction of the apartment but moving out of the city entirely.

'Are you going to tell me where we're going?' She sighed.

'We leave New York tonight,' he said simply.

His silence following the declaration was a reminder of their bargain. No details until they had arrived at their destination. Until she was locked away.

CHAPTER FIVE

THE MIDNIGHT COMMERCIAL flight to Athens provided Priya with a brief reprieve as Eros busied himself with a series of video conference calls and stacks of paperwork emblazoned with that same golden bow and arrow symbol, which she now knew was his company logo. She knew very little about Arcum Investments other than that they were a quiet and predatory investment firm that had swept the European markets over the past decade, but she'd heard tales of their exponential growth and daring risks.

Fitting, she'd thought to herself. Considering she felt like she had been targeted by a hunter. The realisation that she had been cornered so well still stung, but there was no going back now, she thought with ferocity.

The next few weeks would give her the time she needed to regroup and formulate her plans to take her place at the helm of the company she had been born to run. After that, she could sim-

ply pretend that this marriage had never happened until their divorce was finalised. They'd
agreed to a date, one year in the future. One
year and she could forget Eros Theodorou and
forget that kiss.

Three engagements, one wedding and still her
love life was non-existent. Considering her reaction to a simple kiss, she should have tried harder
not to neglect her own needs. She wasn't even
sure if she had any, considering the amount of
contact she'd had with the opposite sex in the
past seven years.

Since her embarrassing public failure of a
wedding to her high school sweetheart, Eric,
she'd avoided all men, which had been easy. Even
when she'd realised she was obligated to feign
a loving marriage with her former groom, she'd
felt nothing. Not even an ember of desire.

One look at Eros Theodorou and it was as
though her poor neglected libido had staged
an outright protest. The moment his lips had
touched hers tonight she had lost all coherent
thought other than *yes* and *more*.

Irritation flared as she realised she had unconsciously raised her fingers to trace her lower
lip as her thoughts whirled. She swore they were
still hot and swollen from his skilful ministra-
tions. A shiver ran down her spine and she forced
herself to keep her gaze focused on the book she

had bought while slowly ambling through the airport stores to avoid her groom.

He may have elicited a response in her, but she knew better than anyone that sexual attraction was easily stirred and discarded.

She would not become one of the notches on his bedpost. He was exactly the kind of man she'd spent her entire life avoiding and now she wore his ring on her finger. Closing her eyes, she tried to focus on the vibrations of the plane around her and not the deep baritone of Eros's voice as he spoke in rapid Greek a foot away from her. She found her eyes drawn to his side of the aisle far too often.

She'd noticed that he was left-handed, and that he kept a small pad of paper just out of sight where she was pretty sure he was doodling. Did billionaire playboys doodle? The thought had made her thoughts wander even more. She'd regain focus on the page once more, only to be distracted again by a loud outburst from his side of the aisle. The man was a force of energy as he worked, constantly moving even while seated.

From the one call he'd taken in English, she'd heard mention of his shares in Mytikas Holdings and a meeting planned, but then he had noticed her attention and moved to the other end of the aircraft. On the next call he'd switched into rapid Greek, but she was sure she'd heard his brother's name mentioned more than once. He used his hands far too much as he spoke, spreading them wide and making gestures that were so thoroughly Mediterranean... Catching her thoughts, she turned away, irritated with herself. He was just a man. A very tall, golden and perfectly structured man but...a mere mortal nonetheless.

Whatever strange stirrings of attraction he'd unlocked within her would have to go unanswered.

She'd managed to drift off into a dreamless sleep at some point, her glasses still on and her book still open on her lap. When she awoke, the cabin was in darkness and someone had reclined her seat and tucked a blanket around her. Her book had been placed on the side table, glasses neatly propped on top.

She looked immediately to her left and found Eros in the same position, his face completely relaxed in sleep.

Somehow she'd slept for almost five hours, almost half the flight time, and the pilot was readying for their descent into Athens. The view from her window showed the late evening sun inching across the ocean below towards the ancient capital city.

When they finally landed and she looked to her side it was to see Eros alert and serious, looking like he'd just stepped off the runway. His blond hair was once again neatly tied back and he had barely a wrinkle in his designer shirt. Meanwhile, she was pretty sure she had mascara clogged under her eyes and the comfortable shift dress and leggings she'd donned for travel were more than a little the worse for wear.

They exited the aircraft first and were met on the tarmac by their own private car. The only time Eros spoke was to explain that he was taking her to his own remote private island and that the only way to get there was via seaplane as the winds were far too treacherous for helicopters. He seemed distracted and suddenly lacking the charming vibrant energy she'd come to expect from him. When they finally arrived at the docks and he stepped onto a small white plane alone, however, she froze.

'Where is the pilot?'

'You're looking at him.' He placed one hand on his hip, his expression hidden behind a pair of mirrored aviator sunglasses. 'Is there a problem?'

'I assume you have a licence?'

'Of course.' He reached into the plane and pulled out a black folder, opening it to reveal some official papers. 'Ten years of experience enough for you?'

She watched as he placed their luggage in the back of the plane himself, noticing that for

'What…? Why?' She half spluttered the words.

'I told you there would be no contact with the outside world.'

Priya turned her face away from him to hide her irritation but as she did so she saw his lips twitch with amusement. Taking a deep breath, she tamped down the urge to turn around and demand to be taken back to the airport. To admit defeat in the face of his shameless attempts to set her off balance.

'If you wanted to lock me away, you could have at least had the decency to do it in a place with an internet connection.'

Eros watched the play of emotions cross over Priya's features and felt the tiniest sprinkling of guilt bubble up to the surface of his long-forgotten conscience. He hadn't thought of this isolation period as locking her away, but now that they had arrived…

He sighed, hefting his case under one arm and watching as she grabbed her own and stalked ahead of him along the whitewashed wooden marina. His reason for waiting until they were already on Greek soil before revealing the truth of their honeymoon was obvious, and judging by the look on her face as she stared out at the endless expanse of sea that surrounded them she had realised that her choices had been effectively limited.

Eros was a man used to getting exactly what he wanted and he had made sure that his bride had absolutely no chance to double-cross him. Of course, if she truly wished to walk away now, he wouldn't stop her. He would take her back to Athens himself, no questions asked. He was not her jailer. But she had agreed to stay by his side until both of their deals were complete and he would not apologise for safeguarding his own interests, considering her track record so far.

He guided her to a wide metal hatch in the rock face and entered a code on the panel by the door. The door slid upward, revealing a deceptively large hangar within that housed a second seaplane and a few smaller electronically powered vehicles.

Eros walked to his sleek white Jeep, which had the fastest land speed, and held the door open, but looked back to see Priya inspecting a small two-seater roadster.

'I have never seen this model. Is it electric?' she asked, running her hand along the hood with obvious reverence.

Eros was curious as he watched her slide her fingers along the seams in the rear of the vehicle and pop the hood to peer inside. 'It hasn't been released yet. I allowed my team to use the island for testing their prototypes. The plane too.'

'You own the brand?'

'I invested in them as a start-up. I liked the idea of cleaner travel between the islands. The land toys were a bonus.'

'They're all electric?' she asked, following the wires to the panel in the wall of rock beside them.

'The island is mostly run on solar and wind, yes.' He walked towards her, looking down at where her delicate hands stroked and prodded at the intricate inner mechanisms of the million-euro toy he'd invested in on a wild hunch. He liked cars—of course he did, he was a red-blooded male—but, unlike a lot of car fanatics he knew, he had very little interest in the actual workings of the vehicles he drove. He was far more interested in the inspiration behind the designs and shape and left the maintenance to his mechanics.

'There isn't really much room in this one for luggage.' He hovered behind her, fascinated at her obvious interest and seeming knowledge.

As though she'd realised he was staring, she straightened and took a step back, popping the hood closed. 'My papa was a classic car collector.'

'I can't imagine you getting your hands dirty,' he mused.

'My mother tried her best to make me into the stereotypical society princess. But Papa told me I could be whatever I wanted to be. I decided I wanted to be…him.' She shrugged.

'Did he put you under all that pressure, or did you do it to yourself?'

She looked up sharply at his words. 'I wanted to work alongside him and join his vision to turn our family's banking empire into a force of good rather than evil.'

Her words stunned him for a moment, a jarring echo of his own youthful self. At twenty-seven she was only seven years younger than him but she was full of positive energy. So seemingly sure of her own path. The urge to tell her about what had brought about his own exile from Zeus's empire rose in him but he pushed it away. This was not some kind of therapy circle.

She didn't need to know about the details of his own naivety, just as she didn't need to know the history that this island held for him. Named Myrtus for its wealth of lush pink Myrtle groves, it had been the only thing left of his stepfather's modest fortune when he'd passed away ten years before. Stavros Theodorou had not been a wealthy man on the scale of Zeus, but he'd done well for himself with some small investments.

When Eros had first returned to Greece, shamed and broken, Stavros had energised him with plans to develop Myrtus into something bigger and better. Community work had been a huge passion of his stepfather's. But then Arcum had come about quickly and the thoughts of revenge had consumed Eros. Every time guilt forced him to cast aside time to come and begin the project, something else had come up. There hadn't been time.

Then Stavros had died and suddenly there had been no rush any more.

As he loaded up the Jeep and they scaled the steep hill that led up to the peak of the island, he felt the history threaten to engulf him.

He had been only five years old when his stepfather had bought the deserted island as a stunning jewel to add to his wife's collection of outlandish gifts. A wife he had continuously tried to bribe with luxurious trinkets and vacations. A woman who had continued to avoid her family in favour of long work trips in faraway countries. Even when she was home, she was never truly present. When Eros had developed a severe stutter, it had been Stavros who had taken him to his various speech therapies. His mother had believed he was fabricating the condition for attention.

By the time he was ten, the only time they ever spent all together was when they were on the island, but by that point every moment had been a strain on his emotional young mind. He had felt every barbed comment and raised voice acutely, and his stutter had reappeared.

It had been here on this island that his mother had served his stepfather with divorce papers. It had been here he had first witnessed the violence that could come from two people with warring hearts. There had never been physical violence but words, in his experience, could be far more deadly. And there had never been a greater weapon in his mother's arsenal than the son Stavros had adored and loved as his own.

In the last days of their marriage, Stavros had thrown party after party to try to lure his wife home to the Greek society she had once loved. But Arista had no interest in being Stavros Theodorou's wife any longer. She had set her sights on a prize far greater.

That final loss had been paralyzing and Eros had watched his stepfather descend into the addiction that had always been there, waiting.

Suddenly this island had become his prison. The place where they'd lived during his designated time with the man who had raised him. Of course his mother had never been allowed to visit.

The affair between Arista and Zeus Mytikas had been whispered about for years until eventually it was revealed she was living with him in

New York. The drama had rocked the tabloids so thoroughly and yet no one had ever suspected that there could be more to the story until it was revealed publicly that Eros was, in fact, Zeus's son. He had always known that Stavros was not his birth father, but it had never bothered him. He had been happy not knowing.

Eros watched as the great white sprawling villa came into view at the southern tip of the island and tried to block out the memory of finding out that his birth father had always known about him, but had paid for his existence to be kept secret from his high society wife. A wife who had finally passed away after a long illness, leaving Zeus childless and in need of heirs.

And nothing had been the same again.

He inhaled the cool salty breeze and tried to feel his stress melt away, annoyed at himself for allowing his thoughts to wander to such darkness. He realised with a frown that Priya had sat like a silent statue beside him for the entire ten-minute journey. She didn't gasp at the views or the stunning wildflower meadows that framed the single winding road that connected the villa to the small bay that housed the marina. He felt the tension rise in him as they passed along the sleek driveway up to the villa. Tall myrtle trees formed orderly sentries along the sides of the neatly maintained avenue.

As the villa came fully into view, like a large white castle atop the highest peak, she didn't comment on the architecture or the stunning views of the bay. With a thoroughly benign expression, she opened her own door once they stopped and took her case out before he had even taken the keys from the engine.

'As far as cages go, it's a pretty beautiful one, don't you think?' she said.

Priya stood in the courtyard and looked up at the most beautiful home she had ever seen. The whitewashed facade was embellished by cascades of pink and purple bougainvillea that covered what seemed to be small turrets at each corner.

She walked through an archway into a sun-drenched courtyard and found herself met by the most stunning view across the Aegean from their high vantage point.

Eros followed close behind her, seemingly annoyed at the fact that she had chosen to take her case herself.

Her muscles felt tight and she was on edge with the effort of watching her every move and word around him. She had to temper her awe-struck reaction to the sight of the most ornate pool she had ever seen in her life. A giant circular shape, the pool was dominated by what looked like an eight-foot-tall sculpture of what appeared to be a nude man, pointing his finger up at the sky. It was an impressive place, and not an unpleasant one in which to spend an extended vacation.

She closed her eyes and pushed away the reminder, not knowing how on earth she would survive one week away from her work, never mind three. She had barely stopped moving over the past few years. Always with her eye on the next goal, the next achievement, the next step towards fulfilling whatever it was that haunted her every moment that she stood still.

Pushing away the suddenly dark turn her thoughts had taken, she waited as Eros unlocked the terrace doors and led her into an impressive open-plan living space.

All the brightness from the outside was mirrored inside with cream-coloured tiles and lush curved sofas, giving the space a modern airy feel yet still having touches that were quintessentially Greek.

The window frames on the inside were the same deep sapphire-blue as they were outside. There were no ultra-modern glass walls here. The house had clearly been renovated at some point in the past few years, yet it remained classically Greek.

She remembered Eros's words about his penthouse in New York, that he liked to keep parts of history and build around them. She might almost begin to think that he was a romantic soul.

'You are quiet.' His deeply accented voice came from behind her.

'Maybe I'm speechless with joy.'

'Quiet and now sarcastic.' He cocked his head to one side, observing her with such intensity it made her skin prickle. 'Just what every groom wants to see from his bride on their honeymoon.'

'I'm just processing things, that's all.' She shook her head, running her finger along a bookcase filled with novels in many languages and ignoring the flutter in her stomach at the thought of being on honeymoon. This wasn't that, certainly not.

'Regretting walking away from your grand society wedding?' His voice was closer, a strange tension in him that made her back away a step.

'I have no regrets.' She steeled herself, straightening her spine as she looked up at him. 'I made my commitment, as did you.'

'You know... I suppose this is technically our wedding night.' He prowled closer, that smirk once again gracing his full lips. 'Perhaps I should have written a romantic island consummation into our contract.'

Priya avoided his eyes. 'I wouldn't have signed

it if you had. I am not the kind of woman easily pulled off course by anyone.'

'Am I so easy to generalise?' He cocked his head to one side, watching her with the shrewd gaze of a hunter. 'Do you often moan into a kiss like you've tasted heaven?'

'Don't flatter yourself.'

'We can try it again if your memory needs refreshing.' His pupils seemed to widen, his eyes lowering to her lips. 'I'd like the chance to sample my beautiful bride in private.'

His words lit up that same spark within her, the needy primal core that she had long buried and suppressed. She was not that girl any more, she didn't long for the protection and security of marriage to the right man. To her, marriage was the opposite of safety. Already she felt vulnerable and on edge just from him saying it out loud.

She had moved so far away from this world. From powerful, overbearing men who believed they knew better than the women they claimed to be in lifelong partnerships with.

Tilting her chin up, she met his eyes and wondered how on earth she'd managed to get herself into this situation. The man was a veritable sexual force of nature and he seemed intent on pushing her out of her comfort zone. She needed to show him that she was not some meek and mild society princess to be manipulated and cowed. She was his wife now, after all.

A shiver coursed down her spine at the thought.

Shocking herself, she took a step forward until barely an inch remained between their chests. Forcing herself to look up, she met his cerulean gaze. 'Allow me to make one thing perfectly clear. I may have agreed to marry you, but I did not suddenly transform into an object that you can own. I am not a pocket watch.'

His eyes gleamed at her words but he did not laugh. Suddenly the air between them was thick and heated. Priya felt too warm and too bare under his gaze. Mustering up the composure for one final supercilious brow rise, she turned away to continue her explorations, feeling the heat of his gaze follow her every step of the way.

CHAPTER SIX

EROS KNEW THAT Priya was lying when she said she was taking a nap a short while later, as she had got what he considered to be a full night's sleep on the last leg of the flight to Athens. He had ensured she was left undisturbed, insisting on checking her comfort himself when the staff had offered to dim the lights in the cabin. He remembered the silky feeling of her hair under his fingertips when he'd accidentally brushed against it while removing her glasses so that they didn't become damaged.

He'd reclined her seat quickly and efficiently after that, eager to step away into his own space. But he'd found his concentration lacking, his eyes continually wandering back to her and her unnatural stillness as she slept.

He'd hoped she might enter into some more verbal sparring and give him another chance to see what was truly going on behind that fiercely intelligent and serious gaze.

He wanted to know more.

The thought stopped him in his tracks, knitting his brows together with almost painful force. Had it truly been so long since he had last blown off some steam in the bedroom that he was lusting after his angry wife? She had openly admitted to despising him, and likely found him lacking compared to his paragon of a brother. That she had ever thought his brother to be some kind of avenging Robin Hood infuriated him even more. He knew that Xander only cared for his bank account and his image, in that order.

Anger fuelled him as he deposited his luggage in the master suite and stepped into the shower, cleaning away the grime of travel with swift, angry strokes. He was becoming soft if one woman's opinion could have such a drastic effect on his mood. He shouldn't care if she liked the damn island.

He walked over to the small urn that sat atop a marble sideboard by the wide windows of the master suite. He had placed it there the day after Stavros's funeral, but then, filled with anger, he'd walked away without truly saying goodbye.

This rock had been his stepfather's prized possession and in his final days he had used it as a prison of his own making. Hiding himself away.

He had often been subjected to his stepfather's drunken diatribes about his wayward wife. He had known far too much at too young an age. Their short marriage had been so unhappy and turbulent that he remembered his relief and happiness when he'd finally found out that they were to be divorced.

His happiness had been short-lived, with him being used as a prize between two hateful and emotionally immature adults during the following years, until he'd eventually turned eighteen. His best interests had always come second to their need for control and revenge against each other. For their need to win their petty battles, not caring that he had grown up in a war zone.

The memories of endless months spent roaming this island alone were particularly difficult to revisit. But he had some happy memories here with his stepfather and this was the place Stavros had requested to be laid to rest.

By now, Arista would be beginning to piece together his double-cross. He almost wished he had decided to give the news in person. Did that make him just as hateful as she was? Perhaps, but every ounce of hate in him had in part been created by her and the choices she'd willingly made.

He walked out into the centre of his bedroom and surveyed his reflection in the mirror. He was only thirty-four but he felt like he had lived two lifetimes already. His father's first, and now his own. If this was his second life, maybe it was time he started doing solely what he wanted. He had told Priya that she could do with time away from the city but the same could also be said for him. He had travelled non-stop over the past few years, expanding his empire. Despite his reputation as a spoilt European party boy, he couldn't remember the last time he had taken a vacation of any kind.

The effort of keeping his transactions away from Mytikas's ears had meant doing much more work in person than would normally be the case for a man of his wealth.

The thought of being forced to stay here for a few weeks in the sun, becoming reacquainted with this little slice of heaven... It was not entirely unappealing.

Except for the fact that his vacation medication came with a guest. A dark, brooding guest who wore his ring on her finger and currently bore *his last name*.

She was just another stuck-up society heiress, he reminded himself. He should hate her and everything she stood for by agreeing to become a part of the obnoxious fake world of corruption and ballgowns that his brother inhabited.

And yet something bothered him deeply about the image she portrayed.

His mind wandered back to that kiss. The pretty cherry flush of her lips afterwards and the dazed sparkle in her chocolate-coloured eyes. Something within him had growled with satisfaction the moment he'd felt her stop holding back. The moment she had broken and acknowledged the intense chemistry between them.

His body instantly reacted to the erotic image his mind created and he hissed out a low breath, fighting the urge to continue the fantasy. His skin felt too hot, every muscle in his body wound tight with tension begging for release. But not just any release. Claiming her. Bringing down those polished stone walls surrounding her and making her completely lose control.

If just thinking of making love to his wife affected him this way...

He walked out onto his balcony, not caring that he wore only a white towel draped low on his hips.

Just a few weeks, he reminded himself. Just a few weeks here and they would part ways and he would be free to go wild and satiate the incurable lust that seemed to hound him of late. Soon he would finally finish snuffing out every last piece of evidence that Zeus Mytikas had walked this earth.

Priya ducked behind the pillar of what she'd believed to be her own private balcony but in fact was an adjoining one to what was evidently her husband's suite. Eros stood half-naked, tilting his head back to the sun like he was playing a part in a damned TV commercial.

She wrenched her gaze away from her husband's impossible beauty, quietly closed her sliding door behind her and promptly threw herself face down onto her bed.

She didn't even have the luxury of screaming her frustrations into her pillow for fear he would hear her and come barging in to investigate. He had deliberately re-awoken the memory of how her body had reacted to their wedding kiss, trying to unsettle her and make her blush. The way he'd looked at her as he'd taunted her had only served to heat her blood more, as though he'd wished to devour her.

The realisation that he was attracted to her too had unlocked some hidden pocket of desire she'd buried deep, deep inside and now she was working furiously to try to gather it all back in before she completely embarrassed herself.

In the few minutes of watching him she'd been amazed at how at ease he was in his own body. She'd seen the smallest lines around his eyes as he exhaled on a long, deep sigh. Smile lines, she'd realised. This was a man who smiled so much they had left a mark on him. What did it feel like to live with that kind of abandon? For as long as she could remember, people had commented on her serious nature. Little girls were supposed to smile, Mama had urged when young Priya had abandoned the delicate country club tea parties in favour of reading or playing billiards with her father.

Her father had always allowed her to be herself, whether they had been working on his classic cars or just sitting reading side by side in the library. His sudden death had hit them all hard.

And as she'd grieved for Papa, she'd bloomed into a young woman and her beauty had become even more notable than her mind. Suddenly Mama's gentle urging her towards members of the opposite sex had become more insistent. She'd thought that it was her way of connecting, that she was simply traditional. But soon it seemed that attracting a suitable man was the only thing they'd talked about and marriage the ultimate achievement. She had no longer been allowed to play billiards or chess or to work on the cars but had been forced to attend feminine etiquette lessons and socialise with the daughters of her parents' wealthy friends. Her clothing had to be pre-approved, and her extracurricular activities cut back in favour of charity dinners and social events.

When she'd met Eric, everything had intensified. What should have been the first flush of innocent teenage infatuation had become a stage production. Both of their parents had pushed for an immediate wedding. She had been eighteen.

Looking back, she had always known there was something more behind her mother's manipulations. On the eve of her wedding day, she'd gone to her father's old office, as she had most evenings. She'd sat in his big leather chair and sobbed, thinking about how much she was missing him and wishing he were still alive to walk her down the aisle. She'd wondered why she felt so confused about something that was supposed to be a joyous occasion. She certainly hadn't felt joy.

Then she'd gone in search of tissues and come across the details of his last will and testament instead. It had all been laid out in black and white. Every last cent of his estate was left to her, including the shares he controlled in Davidson Khan. He'd left everything to her, but had locked it away, tied it up in an ironclad trust until such time as she married or turned thirty.

The last words her mother had ever spoken to her that day, once she'd stopped sobbing and begging her to reconsider calling off the wedding, would be imprinted in her mind for ever.

You will always be alone.

She had been her mother's greatest failure and once Priya had finally accepted that she would never fit into the mould Mama wished for her, she'd stepped into the role of black sheep with gusto. Cut off from all financial help, she'd left for college on her own merit after achieving a scholarship and had never looked back, accepting an internship with a rival firm in New York and throwing herself into the work that she loved.

She flung her arm over her face, feeling exhaustion creep into her bones despite having slept on the plane. She was used to travelling—she'd done a bit after graduation with Aria—but had never been able to truly relax the way her best friend's carefree spirit allowed her to. She'd watched her friend go on dates but she'd had no time for them herself. Once she'd been promoted to associate she'd accepted moves to their foreign offices and made a name for herself as a tireless force—reliable, if a little intense. She'd grown past the boundaries that had caged her in and she'd taken time to figure out who she was.

But, still, as she drifted, her mother's voice remained in the background, reminding her that she had remained alone.

Priya awoke with a start to complete darkness. Frowning, she realised she must have nodded off to sleep at some point. When she checked the slim watch on her wrist she was shocked to realise she had slept for almost four hours. After a quick shower, she dressed in her favourite pair of white skinny jeans and opted for a pale blue blouse that was embroidered with tiny seed pearls around the collar. The resulting look was smart but not too dressy, considering she had no way of knowing what the dress code might be for dinner.

It suddenly dawned on her that she had no idea who would be doing the cooking if there were no staff on the island. The question was answered the moment she entered the large kitchen at the rear of the house.

Eros stood with his back to her, stirring an array of pots and pans on the state-of-the-art cooker.

She cleared her throat so as not to alarm him. 'Do you need any help?'

He tipped his head in her direction as an acknowledgement of her presence. 'Ah, the princess has risen from her slumber at last. You can set the table, if that's not too far below your station.'

'It's almost as though you forget that you too are the heir to a large fortune.'

'Yes, but I find it funny when people comment on my birthright, whereas you get that delightful little bridge between your brows and blow air through your nostrils. Rather like an irritated horse.'

'Horse,' she repeated slowly.

'Stallion, if you prefer.' He raised one brow. 'Yes, more of a stallion than a mare, I believe. Especially if your track record in the boardroom is anything to go by.'

Priya moved to one of the drawers, selecting a tablecloth and an array of utensils before moving over to the large marble table that dominated the dining area. 'You've been investigating my track record?'

'Of course. I could hardly marry a woman without knowing how much worth she had added to her previous employer's value. Isn't that how all great fairy-tales begin?'

Despite herself, she laughed quietly at his words. 'I'm still the princess in this scenario, I presume?'

'Upon reflection, I'm prepared to offer you an apology for my earlier comments about your privileged upbringing and haughty demeanour. In fact, I feel foolish now for not realising you are much more suited to the role of Queen or Empress.'

Priya remained silent as she spread the table-cloth and finished arranging the silverware in preparation for dinner. But she could feel his eyes on her, waiting for her response.

'I assume you are the white knight in this tale.'

'Oh, no,' he said with obvious pleasure as he advanced on her with two steaming plates of food in his hands. 'I'm far too self-centred to be considered a hero of any kind.'

'You are the villain, then.'

'Perhaps. But I've always believed even the villain has his reasons for doing what he does.'

Priya thought on his words for a moment and realised that her own action of jilting her original groom might also be perceived as villainous. It made her feel uncomfortable that people would see her in such a light without knowing the truth behind the story. But wasn't that exactly how she had treated Eros?

Before she could think too much on the topic she was presented with a perfect dish of golden seafood risotto. Delivered fresh by a local fisherman, he explained. Famished, she inhaled the scent of the fresh seafood and herbs and vegetables so vibrant and intensely flavourful they had to have come fresh from the garden.

Neither of them spoke for a while as they tucked into their food. Priya tried to eat slowly but soon she found her plate was completely clear.

'A high society woman with a good appetite,' his voice teased as he leaned down to collect her plate. 'Wonders never cease.'

'Not unlike a billionaire who knows how to cook,' she retorted, mirroring his tone, at which he let out a single burst of laughter.

She suddenly realised with horror that she was quite enjoying his company and that went directly against her plans for this arrangement. It was much easier to keep an enemy at arm's length, despite the sayings to the contrary. He may be her ally in their arrangement, but in every other sense he felt more like a threat. A dangerous force, set on unravelling her orderly world.

He arrived back at the table with a second plate, this time with fresh swordfish and mixed greens. The vegetables were delightfully tender, dressed in a simple olive oil and lemon sauce. Priya fought not to moan with delight at the cavalcade of taste that exploded in her mouth on biting into the fish.

Damn him, she thought mournfully. On top of being blessed with perfect looks, he could also work magic in the kitchen. And not just throwing together a concoction of ingredients and hoping for the best, which was what she usually did. This was the kind of cooking learned from experience and pleasure.

'Where on earth did you find the time to learn how to cook in between being an internationally renowned playboy and founder of a secret empire?' she wondered aloud.

'Now you're really making me sound like a villain.' He smirked. 'I learned to cook here, actually. During my teenage years, I spent a lot of time here. The people who live here and farm the land year-round run a small restaurant on the nearby island. They taught me much of what I know. To fly a seaplane, to make wine and olive oil.'

'Sounds like an ideal childhood,' she said, noting that his expression seemed suddenly darker. 'Do you come back often?'

'Yes, if you can consider every ten years as being often.' He spoke in a gruff monotone.

'Why such a long time if you love the place?'

'My stepfather died here.'

The fleeting haunted look in his eyes was so dark she had to fight the urge to reach out and touch his arm. She knew what it felt like to lose a parent. 'Were you close?'

'Does it matter, once they've passed?' He shrugged, levelling her a crooked half-attempt at a smile that did strange things to her chest. She opened her mouth to ask more but he quickly changed the subject.

When he created two mixed drinks and invited her to follow him out onto the terrace she still felt the urge to prod and poke and find out more, then stopped herself.

Her expression must have shown her own discomfort for when she looked up it was to see him looking right back at her knowingly.

'There is no need to maintain the ice princess facade with me, Priya,' he said coolly. 'I will not jump your bones at the first sign of kindness, if that's what you think.'

'I don't know what to think of you,' she said honestly. 'That's the problem.'

'Why is that a problem?' he asked. 'Do you often need to have precise labels on all the people you are in contact with?'

'When you say things like that...' She looked away towards the moonlight that was gracing the top of the waves with silvery light. Why did he seem to see so much where others had never looked twice? No one had ever asked her why she behaved the way she did. Why she seemed to hold back her emotional reactions in favour of silent reproach. Yet from the first moment they had spoken he had *seen* her. She wasn't quite sure if that realisation made her nervous in reproach or anticipation.

Anticipation of what? she asked herself, pushing the thought away quickly. The only thing that she should expect from this man was deception and manipulation and she would do well not to forget that.

He was a world-class playboy. Working women was quite literally his bread and butter. Already she had fallen into his trap by enjoying his meal and his flirtatious conversation just like any other woman would. Disappointment flooded her at the ease with which she had fallen for it all.

'So serious, Priya,' he said, taking another sip from his drink. 'What terrible things are you thinking about me right now?'

'You are so arrogant that you presume I'm even thinking of you.'

'I presume nothing,' he said quickly. 'I can simply see when you are thinking of me. You get a particular dark look in your eyes and you make sure not to look in my direction. It's quite attractive, actually.'

She felt a flare of temper, her hands tightening on the arms of her chair, but just as she was about to raise her voice in reproach she noticed the mirth sparkling in his eyes. He was enjoying every single moment of this. Damn him. Taunting her simply to get a reaction.

'This will be a very long three weeks if that's the best you can do.' She spoke with deliberate calmness, sitting back in her seat and taking a long, languorous sip of her drink, licking the sugar from the corner of her lips, his eyes following the movement.

'You are accusing me of playing games again.'

'Aren't you?' she asked, stifling a yawn behind her hand.

To her pleasure she could see the smallest

tightening around his lips. He thrived on her reaction and so logically her lack of reaction would
be torturous.

Perhaps she was putting far too much stock in
his investment in antagonising her for sport, but
she was good at reading people, she always had
been. Except when it came to the ones she loved,
a small voice said. She pushed it away.

In business, she could read people. She could
tell by his body language that he was barely holding onto his control. One foot tapped idly on the
floor as he swirled the liquid in his glass. He
was looking away from her, probably trying to
come up with a different angle from which to
prod. The interactions were not unlike fencing,
both parrying, stepping back and then edging
forward, waiting for the right moment to strike.

CHAPTER SEVEN

EROS MEASURED HIS words before he responded, wondering why her stony exterior bothered him quite so much.

He had met plenty of women in his life who pretended to be one thing when in fact they were another, his mother being the prime example. But that was not it. He didn't care that his mother pretended to be kind on the outside when underneath she was far from it.

But with Priya he felt the compulsion to tap at that suit of armour she insisted on wearing to show her that he saw through the layer of perfectly polished ice she presented to the world. To see how far he could push to get a glimpse of what lay beneath.

'Does my attention make you uncomfortable?' he asked, gauging her reaction and knowing that if she said yes he would stop.

She looked away, hiding her expression behind the curtain of her long brown hair.

'It's inappropriate.'

'That was not my question.'

She turned and pinned him with a sharp gaze, amber eyes burning in the candlelight, and he was struck by arousal so intense it took his breath away. What would it be like to unleash that fire? What would it be like to let her burn him in it?

Almost as though he had spoken out loud, her eyes darkened and almost as if against her own volition, her tongue darted out to explore her bottom lip in a quick lick.

He felt that lick deep in his gut and lower, taunting him with the sight of her perfectly pink tongue and the glistening trail it left on her full pouting lips. When she looked at him like that, he knew he wasn't mistaken.

She had said that their relationship was to remain strictly business and he respected that but he didn't believe that was what she truly wanted.

'I am not the kind of man to play games where it counts, Priya. If I behave as though I am attracted to you it's because I am. Very much so.'

She inhaled a sharp hiss of breath, but did not cut him with a sharp retort. So, the direct approach had got her attention. He would remember that. He sat forward, placing his elbows on his knees and looking up at her from under his brows.

It was the kind of look he normally reserved

for a date when he wanted things to move further. A smouldering look that usually had an intense and sudden effect on the woman he directed it upon.

Priya bit down on her lower lip, displaying the tiniest flash of her white teeth as she held back whatever words she had been about to speak.

Tell me, he silently urged, then felt irritation flare as he watched her shrink back.

'Does that usually work?' she said breathlessly, trying and failing to appear unmoved. She gestured to her face and made an impressive attempt at imitating his expression.

Eros froze for a split second, then almost lost his composure completely, his mouth cracking into the barest smirk.

'Yes, it does, as a matter of fact.'

She pressed a hand to her chest with a dramatic flourish. 'I'm honoured to be the recipient of such esteemed moves.'

'Yet you are completely immune?' he asked silkily.

She ignored his question. 'Be serious for a moment. Tell me that you don't see how utterly inappropriate all of this is.'

Eros sat back in his seat and shrugged one shoulder. 'Tell me to stop.'

'Stop,' she said quickly, still not meeting his eyes.

'Say it as if you actually mean it. Say it as if

you haven't thought of what might happen if you let loose and had some fun. It could be just the kind of distraction that we both need.'

'I know how to have fun,' she protested.

'You are wound up so damn tight...' He let heat burn in his gaze as he leaned forward. 'One night in my bed, Priya... I swear I wouldn't stop until we were both boneless from pleasure.'

Her eyes widened. Her breathing became shallow and he could have sworn she blushed.

'If you're not going to steer away from this conversation, then allow me to do it for both of us.'

She stood from her seat and looked down at him with her best reproachful glower.

Eros stood too, instantly regretting pushing her so far when he saw the slight tremor in her hands. Whether it was a tremor of arousal or of discomfort he couldn't know. He caught her hand to stop her from retreating from him.

'This place turns me into a slightly darker version of myself and I apologise,' he said with complete sincerity, hating the guarded look that he had put on her beautiful face. 'If you want this to remain a strictly business arrangement, you have my word I will not bother you with any unwanted advances.'

'You seem to view flirtation as a sport,' she said, pulling her hand from his grip.

'You have my word it won't happen again.' She nodded once and he released her, taking a step away before he spoke. 'However, if you change your mind, let me know.'

'About one night of mindless pleasure?'

'It could be mutually beneficial.' He shrugged. 'No strings, no complications.'

She shook her head in disbelief. 'There I was thinking you were actually offering me a sincere apology.' Before she disappeared, she turned back once. 'Hell would freeze over before I accepted the position of night-time distraction in your bed.'

'Well, when you put it like that it doesn't sound—' he began, but quickly realised he was speaking to thin air as she had disappeared inside the house.

That had gone just about as well as he thought it would go.

He wanted her and had made that very clear from the outset. But what he could offer her was not exactly enough to risk putting a strain on their relationship and they both knew that. Still, the idea that she could so easily feign disinterest irked him.

Because *he* was distracted by her presence. And he was never distracted by women. He adored making love with them and he was always respectful when the arrangement came to an end. But his arrangements had never lasted more than a few weeks. Had never involved being trapped alone on an island together.

And none of those women had been his wife.

Business bargain or otherwise, the fact that they had made vows to one another certainly complicated things so he needed to get hold of himself. He would not proposition her again, he had made that promise. But if she came to him?

If she let those walls down and decided she wanted to explore the attraction between them as badly as he did, he wasn't so sure he could say no. And that bothered him most of all.

Priya awoke to the sound of rhythmic banging, as if someone was pounding a hammer against the side of her bedroom wall. For a moment she was disorientated, squinting at the dawn light through the curtains.

The pounding sound stopped, only to start up again. More furious with more power. She quickly rose from bed and moved to the French doors, which she had left slightly ajar to combat the heat. The house did not have air-conditioning, simply large fans in each room and an airy layout.

She opened the doors and stepped out onto the terrace, taking a quick peek to the side to make sure her handsome neighbour was not also investigating. She didn't think she could stand another view of his perfect just-out-of-bed appearance.

But the sight that met her was even more intense. Her husband stood waist deep in the ornamental fountain with a large tool in his hand that looked suspiciously like a sledgehammer, which he was swinging in perfect strokes at the tall statue that stood in the middle.

With each arc, the muscles on his back rippled and sweat glistened on his golden skin.

Priya was entranced, her mouth going dry as she watched the unbelievable spectacle unfolding before her. For a moment she didn't even care why he was destroying what might possibly be a priceless piece of history at dawn, all she could do was watch helplessly as he unveiled the sheer devastating power of his body.

Then he paused, turning to look up at her. Their eyes met and what she saw in his gaze shocked her.

He looked like he was in pain.

Not the kind of physical pain that came from over-exerting oneself or pulling a tendon. It was as though some of his armour had come apart and she had seen through to a place she was never meant to see. He looked away quickly, a charming smile appearing on his face as he turned back and saluted her like a general with his free hand.

'*Kalimera!*' he shouted up to her.

She waved once, then moved back inside to puzzle over what she had just witnessed.

She was still trying to make sense of it by the time she had showered, dressed in olive-green shorts and a black tank top, and gone into the kitchen to see about breakfast.

Already set, the table on the terrace over-looked the sea. Her view of the destruction in the fountain was conveniently blocked by a low wall. But when she closed her eyes, she could still see the ferocious swing of his arms as he beheaded the statue and hear the guttural grunt that came from him.

'I don't remember ordering a wake-up call,' she said dryly as he walked towards her. 'I assume it was part of the plans you mentioned.'

'It was more of an impromptu task,' he said without much emotion. 'I apologise for the timing. I didn't realise it would be so loud.'

'It's fine. I had plans to get up early anyway to get started on my reading.'

'You remember our bargain?'

'I'm not planning to work. It's been a long time since I allowed myself to simply read for pleasure. I grabbed a few books at the airport and that is the full extent of my plans for the next few weeks.' She didn't mention the fact that she'd already constructed a book review tally in her planner complete with goals for maximum pages read per day. Self-consciously she tucked the personal folder further under her chair cushion.

'I'm glad to hear it,' he murmured, seemingly distracted as he stared out at the horizon. She realised he seemed different this morning. Dark shadows circled his eyes and she wondered if he had slept, then reminded herself that that was none of her business. The fact that he showed none of his usual charm and flirtation was disarming but she wouldn't rule out this being another part of his act.

She made some further attempts at banal conversation but when he politely excused himself for some business calls on his own personal satellite connection, she was almost glad to be left alone. She momentarily mourned the loss of her own mobile device but the island had no mobile service so it wasn't like she could have done much. But without the rhythm of her own schedule and goals, she felt rather adrift.

Once she'd cleared away the breakfast dishes, she took the time to explore the rest of the house that she had missed the day before. She found herself charmed by the bright interior decor and soft furnishings. Every room seemed to have a stunning view, whether it was of the pool area and the sweeping views of the Aegean or the large expanse of agricultural land that spread out behind the house like a cape of verdant green.

The sweet, spicy scents of fruit trees and the olive and myrtle groves seemed to come in through every window, mingling with the salty ocean breeze. Eros had mentioned that the house-keepers produced olive oil and she found a door leading down to a large wine cellar filled with barrels of aging wine and tall glass jars of oils and preserves.

Stairs led up from the cellar out onto a covered veranda with a homely wooden dining table covered in small tools and baskets. It was a working area but also an ideal shady spot for a nap, as was evidenced by the large hammock that had been stretched between two pillars.

It was truly like stepping back in time to a simpler pace. She ambled along the cobbled path that led back to the front of the house, inspecting all the beautiful trails of bougainvillea and jasmine that covered the whitewashed facade of the villa, inhaling their aroma and glorying in the vibrant colours.

The heat of the sun on her skin was an instant mood lifter and as she inhaled and exhaled a long breath while staring out at the waves crashing on the cliffs below, she tried to encourage serenity to settle over her. Without her phone and laptop as a distraction she felt both relaxed and strangely adrift in the moment.

Wooden steps had been built into the cliff face leading down to a viewing deck suspended just above the shoreline. The beach here was far too rocky and wild to walk along safely so she settled for spreading out her towel on the wooden planks and settling into the strange and wondrous world that existed in her novel. She had always loved fantasy adventures but once work had become a priority, leisure time had seemed non-existent.

It seemed her brain had lost its ability to concentrate on anything other than investment portfolios. Silence had always been her enemy and she felt the worries of reality looming over her like a cloud, threatening to rain at any moment. Standing up with sudden frustration, she grabbed a handful of rocks and threw them, one by one, into the water. Watching the ripples pass slowly along the surface, spreading out to disturb the previous stillness.

Unlike this barely moving sea, she had always needed a riot of waves and movement to feel anything close to calm. She felt like a ripple moving slowly in reverse, edging backwards from control into the darker corners of her mind where she tried not to look.

What happened when that ripple turned into a swirling whirlpool?

She sat down, hugging her knees to her chest, and tried to push away her visions of the water growing dark, pulling her downward into the fathomless sea of her own thoughts.

Eros continued his demolition over the next few days, only coming back into the house for meals and sleep. The manual work became a burning drive within him, almost as though he was finally keeping the promises he'd made so many years ago. It wasn't enough to undo his wrongs, but it helped with the guilt. Already plans had begun to form in his mind for how he could expand the current architecture to create Stavros's vision. It would be a huge undertaking, but it would be worth it.

If his icy bride was annoyed by his abandonment she did not mention it. In fact, she seemed to disappear entirely during the day, only resurfacing at mealtimes. He had expected a woman who'd grown up in upper-class New York to be unfamiliar with the kitchen, which she was. But, to his surprise, she had found cookbooks and insisted on trying her hand. Again, with that intense focus of hers. Other than mealtimes, the only other time he saw her was when she was in the pool.

He had tried not to look, truly he had. But it was utterly scandalous how she could make her one-piece swimsuits look quite so...sensual. It was the racer back, he decided late one afternoon at the end of their first week as he watched her toned curves cut gracefully through the water. She was all ruthless efficiency, her long limbs powering her body up and down the Olympic-length pool. He'd bet she was even timing herself. Sure enough, as she lifted herself up easily onto the ledge, she picked up the slim gold watch, which she'd left on a nearby table, and a scowl of frustration turned her full lips downward.

He fought the urge to laugh, but still she looked up as though she'd heard his thoughts. One hand moved to her hip and the challenge in her eyes was palpable as she stared him down. He allowed himself one final long, languorous look at her in all her glory before he raised his coffee cup in salute and turned to head back to his work.

He was busy cutting down trees at the rear of the property when he felt a strange prickling on the back of his neck. He turned to find Priya standing under the covered veranda, watching him. The setting sun cast an orange glow over her, illuminating the plain white tank top she wore.

'Do you need help?' she asked quietly. 'I'm not much of a gardener but I'm sure I could be relied on to rip up some plants with enthusiasm.'

'Bored, princess?' He wiped some of the sweat from his brow with his forearm, feeling a pleasurable burn in his shoulders from the labour.

'If you're going to be like that…' She shrugged and turned to take a few steps towards the cobbled path that led out into the manicured gardens.

'Wait.'

She paused, looking back at him over one newly bronzed shoulder. The look of cool challenge on her proud features was strangely alluring. He almost felt bad about how hard a time he'd been giving her. Almost.

'As a matter of fact, I am bored.' She crossed her arms and turned to face him head on. Even with the space of a few metres between them he could see the flecks of gold sparking in her dark eyes.

He smirked with his usual charm, noticing the stiffness in her shoulders relax a little as he did so. He closed the space between them with a few easy strides, pulling off his thick work gloves with two sharp tugs. When he reached out for her hands, she instinctively pulled away and he almost growled with annoyance at the telling movement.

'Put them on.' He grunted and turned to walk back to the wild section of the garden he'd been clearing.

'What exactly is it that we are doing here?' she

asked breathlessly after a while, taking a step back to wipe away some of the perspiration that had gathered on her forehead.

'This was Stavros's favourite part of the garden.'

'Your stepfather?' she asked with a hint of softness.

Eros heard the change in her tone and fought not to roll his eyes. 'Stavros Theodorou was the only father I knew. But yes.'

'How did he die?'

He heard her question but chose not to answer it. The only answer he could give her would be a lie and he did not want any more lies between them.

He could not tell her the truth. He had protected Stavros's reputation for many years and would not stop now.

'I'm sure he would be very proud of your work on the house.'

Eros felt a cruel sound slip from his lips. 'He probably wouldn't care. He hated this place as much as I did towards the end.'

'Is that why you destroyed the statue?' She paused, shaking her head. 'I'm sorry, I'm just trying to make sense of it.'

He paused for a moment, fighting the urge to simply walk away from the conversation as he usually did when it was a subject he did not like.

Childish, perhaps, but that was the way he was. But something in her eyes made him stay.

'The statue was a wedding gift from Zeus,' he gritted, hefting a large rock out of his way. 'He liked to play games. Stavros never suspected.'

'You are doing all this work yourself. You must have loved him.'

'I did, yes.' He cleared his throat. 'Does the fact that I possess a conscience surprise you?'

'Strangely, no. I know that you have an honourable streak. You wouldn't have married me otherwise.'

'I married you mainly for my own purposes,' he said gruffly, hefting the sack over his shoulder and moving across to the small pile he'd accumulated. The physical work had been therapeutic and necessary but he felt like with each swing of his hammer he was uncovering more of the childhood self he'd locked away here.

'The garden will be the only piece of this house that remains once I'm finished.' He spoke the words and watched them register on her face. Saw the frown settle between her perfectly plucked brows as she turned to look up at the historical facade of the villa.

'You can't mean…'

'That I plan to demolish the entire place? Does that surprise you?'

She was quiet for a long moment. Her hands

continued to move as she cut and pruned along a particularly difficult patch of vines that covered the wall. When she spoke, her voice was deliberately calm and devoid of the emotion he realised he suddenly wanted. He wanted her to rise to him and challenge him. Tell him how terrible and selfish his plans were. To shame him just as he constantly shamed himself.

'Ah, there is no sentimentality to it after all,' she mused, half to herself. 'What do you plan to do with it?'

'Redevelop. Capitalise.' He shrugged.

'Just what this part of the world needs. Another luxury resort.'

He did not reply or attempt to put her straight. He simply stood facing her, fascinated by the play of emotions across her face as she tried and failed to disguise the obvious anger growing within her.

'You said you missed this place. Clearly there's history here, anyone could see it in the way you describe the land.'

'Priya, I don't live in the past, I move to the future. It's simply another asset that I acquired along the way.'

'Do you view everything that you acquire so coldly? Because if that's true, perhaps I should fear ruin too.'

He stepped closer, deliberately lowering his

voice. 'The only kind of ruin that I would offer you is the kind that you would beg me for.'

She inhaled one sharp breath. Her amber eyes widened and her pupils dilated. 'I beg no one.'

'I believe you,' he purred, 'but I have never been able to back away from a challenge. You see, here's another secret about me... I despise being told no.'

'That's not a secret.' Her voice was barely a whisper now and there was barely an inch separating their bodies as they stood in the midday heat.

There were no shadows here. Nowhere to hide, only blistering sunlight making his skin feel even hotter than it already felt in her presence. The thrill of seeing her reaction to him made it even harder for him to concentrate on his side of their dance.

Distraction, his mind screamed. That was all this was. A delicious game to occupy himself while they were both forced to stay here together.

The memory of her lips under his had been the last thing he'd thought of every night since they'd arrived on this island. Knowing that she slept on the other side of the wall had tortured him as he had gritted his teeth and taken more than one cold shower or swim in the middle of the night to try to rid himself of the restless energy that had plagued him.

He was not alone in this. Every single day he had seen her walking the length and breadth of the small harbour below the house.

For a woman who had talked about wanting to lie back with a book and switch off, she had done no such thing. She was always moving, cleaning—more than once he'd wandered into the kitchen to find drawers rearranged. She was so wound up she was practically thrumming with excess energy. That, he could help with.

'If I kissed you right now...what would you do?' he asked on impulse.

She didn't answer him immediately, her eyes lowering to his lips before they lifted to meet his gaze. 'Eros...'

'How about now?' He stepped forward another inch. 'If I stopped right here, would you beg me to continue?'

'If anything, it seems like you would be the one to beg me,' she said breathlessly.

'You would like that, wouldn't you?' He fought the urge to move closer, knowing there was a delicate balance to their game. 'Tell me, are you imagining it right now?'

She bit her lower lip, her eyes glazing over slightly, and he became instantly hard at the idea that she might be fantasising about exactly what he was. She was quiet for a moment and he briefly contemplated simply closing the gap between them, everything be damned.

In the end, she made the decision for him, leaning forward and pressing her mouth tentatively to his.

CHAPTER EIGHT

PRIYA HAD APPROXIMATELY ten seconds of holding the upper hand before Eros growled under his breath and pulled her closer. Her own tentative kiss was commandeered and guided into a red-hot meeting of tongues and teeth that made her cheeks heat and her heart pump wildly in her chest. His big hands moved down to splay across her hipbones, his grip tight and unyielding, holding her in place.

The rest of their surroundings fell away into the background and she was immersed in him. In his scent and his heat and the delicious taste of wine on his tongue. She thought she had kissed in the past, thought she had been kissed. But there was no comparison.

The kiss was the most wonderful, terrible thing she'd experienced. She scrambled to keep her thoughts straight, to remind herself of all the reasons why this was a terrible idea, but it was useless. She felt control slipping through her fingers with each slide of his tongue against hers. She melted into him, giving in to the roar of arousal in her ears and the tightening of need building within her.

'You taste amazing.' His voice was a husky murmur against her lips as he proceeded to quite literally taste her with a slide of his tongue. The sensation sent a jolt of heat between her legs and she squeezed her thighs together with shock.

His lips continued in their passionate onslaught, stoking the fire within her out of control. It was too much, she thought desperately. He was too much. He was a bona fide playboy and if he had any idea how inexperienced she truly was...

As though he sensed her inner battle, he pulled back and met her gaze. 'What's wrong?'

Priya could have laughed at the absurdity of the moment if she wasn't so mortified. What would he say if she told him that actually she was so anxious about the idea of her own sexual performance, she was on the verge of a panic attack. The intimacy of the moment was too much. She was too warm and too out of breath and she needed to think.

His breath fanned her cheek, his hands still splayed against her bare skin, and she felt the urge to just lean back in, to dive back into the pleasure he was stoking and try to ignore all the rest of the thoughts swirling in her mind.

But she knew too well her mind didn't work like that.

Pressing two hands against his chest, she gave a gentle push while simultaneously moving backwards. 'This is a terrible idea.'

'It didn't feel terrible to me.'

'You know what I mean, Eros.' She blew out a long breath, focusing on the hum in her chest as a centring point. 'I don't want to be a part of your games, or whatever this is.'

'That's what you think of me?' His expression became dangerously calm as he surveyed her. 'You think this is another part of my revenge?'

'Maybe.' She shrugged. 'You said yourself not to trust you.'

'Do you wish you'd married him instead, Priya?' he murmured with exaggerated softness. 'Would you have preferred to have him kissing you into oblivion right now?'

She didn't answer the question, feeling the tension emanate off his bare shoulders in waves. She couldn't even have pictured any other man's face right now if a million dollars had been on the line. All she could see and feel was Eros. If this was a part of his plan, he was an incredible actor. Suddenly she knew why she was so afraid of how he made her feel. Because for the first time in her life she knew what she wanted. Too bad that it was the one thing she couldn't allow herself to take.

Eros walked away from her and sat back in one of the large lounge chairs under the covered veranda. Tension still rolled off his powerful shoulders in waves, but he didn't look up at her.

'Goodnight,' she murmured, walking back up the steps into the house and resisting the urge to look back. Every step seemed to tighten the knot in her chest even further, the familiar burn creeping into her lungs. The climb up to her bedroom may as well have been a hike up Mount Olympus for the state it put her in.

Panic crowded her thoughts, tightening her limbs and limiting her breathing. Her fingers shook as she reached for her small medicine case. She had once resisted the idea of needing any help to manage her anxiety when it took over this way, seeing it as a weakness. Aria had been the one to make her seek help when intense college deadlines and her fragile relationship with her mother had brought her to her knees.

Now she saw her medication for what it was, a lifeline.

Spreading her blankets on the floor, she lay down and breathed deeply. She'd done enough therapy by now to know exactly why she had reacted this way, but still she asked herself the same question over and over for the next few hours until she fell into a fitful sleep.

Why had she kissed him?

But most of all, why had he been so angry when she'd stopped?

Eros woke with a start, the echoes of a woman's cries in his ears.

He allowed himself a moment for his eyes to adjust to the faint light filtering in through the open balcony doors. The air was still and silent. The sun had not yet risen into the sky but he could see the glowing blush of pink along the horizon.

Everything seemed well and yet... He watched the linen curtains blow in the gentle breeze and tried to pinpoint what had awoken him. Some inner pull had him rising from his bed and walking out onto the terrace as though he knew what he would find there.

He almost didn't see the small shape huddled up on one of the lounge chairs. Priya lay there, a blanket wrapped around her. For a moment he wondered if she had fallen asleep in such an uncomfortable position, but then her eyes opened, their brown depths so haunted it stopped him still in his tracks. She quickly recovered her expression, but he had got a glimpse under the mask for that split, unguarded second and he burned to reach out for her. To chase away those shadows in the only way he knew how.

The thought jarred him with its intensity.

'Is everything okay?' He kept his distance, remembering her words from the night before. Still, the tell-tale redness around her eyes and on the tip of her nose made something tense within him.

'My body clock is used to rising before dawn.' She shrugged. 'It's a good excuse to watch the sun rise every morning. It's…relaxing.'

'You don't look relaxed.'

'I'm fine,' she said quickly, standing up and folding the blanket into a neat square, then worrying at the corners.

He gently took the blanket from her hands, waiting until she finally met his eyes.

'I'd like the truth now. Are you so unhappy here?'

She shook her head and for a moment he wondered if she might simply walk away, back into her bedroom, and lock him out once more. It shouldn't matter to him if she kept her walls up even when she was suffering. He shouldn't care.

And yet he did.

When she finally sighed and turned back towards him, he felt a rush of triumph.

'This island is beautiful.' She shook her head, shrugging one soft shoulder. 'It's just so…quiet.

I've never coped well without keeping busy. I need constant motion.'

'Like a shark,' he mused, smirking when he saw the frown lines appear between her eyes. 'Sharks need to keep swimming continuously—if they stop, they die.'

Her gaze brightened up slightly. 'So I'm a shark now? How flattering.'

Eros knew exactly how it felt to feel utterly adrift in one's own thoughts. She openly admitted to being a workaholic, to filling in her days with projects and goals. When was the last time that she had truly stood still? Suddenly an idea took hold.

'You said you like tasks and hard work?' he asked, watching as her eyes brightened and she nodded quickly. 'How quickly can you have an overnight bag packed?'

Within the hour, Eros had driven them down to the pier and they set sail on a sleek white yacht. She looked over her shoulder, taking in the verdant green jewel that was the island disappearing into the distance behind them. All that claustrophobia and anxiety seemed to melt away with every metre they moved forward through the crystal blue waters.

Eros seemed practised and knowledgeable as he pointed out the various other small islands dotted around them and explained that fishing was strictly limited to certain areas to protect the environment. As the sun began to rise higher in the sky, turning the dawn light pink and purple in the clouds, he brought them to a stop.

They both took a moment to simply breathe. It was impossible not to be enchanted by the stillness of the water and the complete lack of a breeze in the air. But instead of feeling claustrophobic in the absence of hustle and bustle, she felt strangely at ease. Gulls cried overhead, flying in the race to find their breakfast.

Instead of taking charge of the fishing part of the trip, Eros was surprisingly patient as he explained the difference between hooks and bait rods and reels and other terminology that she had heard previously but never actually given much thought to.

Once he had set her up with her own line, he moved to a spot at the rear of the boat and their small talk soon turned to silence. The kind of easy, companionable silence she had never truly experienced with another person. She no longer saw him in black and white, she realised. He was no longer an enemy. Yet she did not think of him as a friend, did she?

He had seen the anxiety rising in her and instead of commenting on it he had expertly redirected her attention. He had given her exactly what she needed without expecting anything in return.

She would only be lying to herself if she said that she hadn't replayed that kiss in her head over and over again since yesterday but she still knew that it had been a mistake that could not be repeated.

She stole a glance at him every now and then, watching the delicate play of his muscles as he easily managed all the various instruments. He seemed to be an expert. She, on the other hand, achieved nothing. No surprise really, considering the first time something pulled at her line she had immediately squealed and almost let the entire rod disappear into the water.

Thankfully Eros had quick reflexes and was right there when she needed him. He capably rescued the fishing rod, inadvertently grabbing her, as well.

'I would never have thought such a sound could come from such a serious, dignified woman.'

'I am still dignified,' she said quickly. 'I just have a severe dislike of surprises. All of this would be much more efficient if we could schedule the fishing. What's the point in getting up and going out at dawn with no guarantee of getting anything?'

'Oh, yes, the perfect plan. Unfortunately, the

ocean does not abide by a timetable and I am unable to pre-order fish at this time.'

She tried to stifle her smile but of course he saw it.

'Did you just respond to my humour?' he purred sulkily, his blue eyes glinting in the sunlight. 'Anyway, speak for yourself, I've already got five fish.'

'What?' She walked over to his bucket and sure enough inside there were five large fish, already gutted and cleaned.

'This is ridiculous.' She sighed, moving to slap herself back down on her own bench and glower at her empty bucket.

'I imagine this is that competitive nature I've read so much about.'

'I like to succeed. Is that another strike on my score sheet?'

'You think I award women scores according to their attributes?'

She frowned. 'I think anyone is lying if they say that they don't have traits that they admire or dislike in another person.'

'And you see your competitiveness as a trait to be disliked?'

'In my experience, men prefer women to be quietly efficient. We are allowed to be capable and to progress but we are not allowed to impinge on another person's success.'

'By another person you mean a man.'

Priya didn't answer his question. She simply raised her eyebrows and went back to focusing on casting her line out again. She would catch a fish today if it killed her. Even if it was only to wipe that satisfied smirk off his face. She felt him move and sit beside her on her bench, leaning over just a fraction to expertly angle her rod in the way he had done the first time. She was grateful for the fact that rather than taking her rod or moving his hands over hers, he simply sat back and gave short clipped instructions.

He praised her efforts when she finally did it correctly and didn't so much as blink when she almost let the rod go again at the first hint of a tug. The low rumble of his voice moved closer to her ear.

'Easy now. You've got it.'

And sure enough she had. She had caught her first fish. Unabashedly she pumped her fist in the air and did a little shimmy of a dance.

'I did it! I actually caught one.' Then she dipped and carefully dropped her bounty into her bucket.

She turned to face Eros. He had the strangest look on his face and Priya felt suddenly self-conscious. She had an overwhelming urge to simply throw her arms around him. Then he stood and looked at her with such intensity and heat she felt a flush run from her toes right up to her cheeks.

'You are magnificent.'

'It was just one tiny fish.' She looked away, focusing on cleaning her hands. She felt a tension in the air that made her anxiety rise but not in the way it had before. This was a different kind of tension. Tension that came from desire. She was almost afraid to look back up at him, knowing that if there was even the slightest hint of heat there she would give in helplessly. Thankfully he moved back to his own side of the boat and set about clearing up the fishing tackle.

Priya thought of returning to the big echoing glass villa and the endless hours spent alone with her thoughts. It was a beautiful place but it was the kind of slow-paced life that only seemed to send her thoughts into a tailspin. She was enjoying the freedom of being out on the water and having some purpose.

'Are you ready for a little more adventure in your life?' He surprised her, coming to a stop by her side.

She looked up at him, seeing that delicious dimple appearing in his cheek. That little dip of mischief as he set about steering the boat towards a cluster of islands in the far distance.

'I prefer to wing it without a schedule. Are you sure you trust me, princess?'

The nickname reminded her of that first moment in the limo and how utterly infuriated she had been by this ruthless charmer...but hearing it on his lips now didn't have the same effect. In fact, it did the opposite, warming something deep inside her.

'I trust you, Eros.'

She aimed for the words to sound playful but somehow they settled heavily between them. Did she trust him? Just for today or did she truly trust him? When had that happened?

Not wanting to examine that feeling too closely, she settled back into the seat as Eros took command of the helm and they set off across the waves once more.

CHAPTER NINE

HE TOOK THEM along a scenic route that wove around a cluster of islands that speckled the Aegean Sea like golden nuggets. As they neared one of the smaller ones he surprised her by pulling in to a picturesque fishing harbour. The harbour was lined with colourful houses and dominated by a large white church at the centre.

'Welcome to Halki,' Eros's voice rose above the waves. 'The tiniest jewel in the Dodecanese Islands.'

Charmed, Priya felt like she was entering an old vintage movie as she wandered down the cobbled streets of the bustling harbour. Several quaint tavernas looked out onto the sea and after a brief wander around the town, Eros pointed towards a restaurant for lunch.

Priya looked down at her shorts and tank top combo and groaned. 'I'm really not dressed for a restaurant.'

'Dimitri would not care if you were nude, he lives for tourists. They don't get enough here.'

Eros guided her inside, greeting the restaurant owner like an old friend and presenting him with the small container of fish they had caught that morning. They took their seats on the outside terrace. She looked around and noticed the place was surprisingly quiet for Greece at the end of the summer.

'It's nice that you still know the locals, even though you haven't been here in so long.'

He looked away from her to where a fishing boat was unloading its catch.

'I haven't been back to Myrtus for ten years but I have a home here on Halki that I visit often. There was a pretty bad storm a few years back and I paid for a lot of the restoration work. Well, my stepfather's charity did, technically. Stavros was born and raised here and he was very passionate about giving aid to the smaller island communities. With such large tourist resorts scattered around, other places can really suffer.'

'That seems strange considering a large portion of your wealth comes from such large resorts.'

'I like to restore a little balance wherever I can. There is a place for my resorts and building developments but I try to make sure that my plans never take away from the existing surroundings.'

Priya was quiet for a moment, almost wanting to bite her tongue at the question she knew she needed to ask. 'So why do you insist on destroying a place you clearly adore? It has plagued me from the moment we arrived. You clearly have a beloved history on Myrtus. I just want to understand.'

For a moment, she worried that he might simply ignore her question.

'Perhaps I was not entirely honest when I told you of my plans for the island. But, you see, explaining the truth would require me to betray a trust that I long ago swore to protect. But I suppose that trust is no longer needed once I go through with my plans so perhaps it's time that I shared it.'

'Eros, I didn't mean for you to—'

'No, it's fine,' he said quickly. 'It hasn't sat right with me that you believe me to be such a cruel and callous capitalist. The truth is I don't plan to turn the island into a resort at all. It is to become a retreat centre.'

He thought back to that time in his life and even though it had been a decade since Stavros's passing, he still felt that helplessness. His stepfather's alcoholism had been nothing compared to the other invisible battle that had been waged within him every day. He had told himself that he was preserving his anonymity by not visiting and allowing him to lock himself away on the island.

But really he had simply abandoned him like an unwanted problem.

When Stavros had eventually passed away, Eros had been hundreds of miles away at a week-long event in the Côte d'Azur.

Brushing off that memory, he looked back at the woman in front of him, so curious and so gentle.

'I have often heard of luxury treatment centres for addicts or even yoga retreats but I want to create a place of true retreat. Accessible to the public, but private for those who need the privacy.'

'That's beautiful, Eros.'

'Don't mistake me for a complete altruist,' he said quickly. 'I will obviously be charging exorbitant fees to any celebrities who need that anonymity.'

'I bet you don't plan on keeping that profit, though, do you?'

'You're trying to read me again, I take it,' he said quickly, taking a large sip of his ouzo. 'I am a puzzle that no woman has ever successfully solved.'

'Are you issuing a challenge?'

Was he imagining it or did he see a slight spark of interest in that dark gaze? He had thought he'd seen something in her eyes when they had been on the boat, but he'd assumed it was a remnant of whatever had plagued her in the early hours of the morning. But now, looking at her closely, he saw the tell-tale widening of her pupils and the way her tongue crept out to gently moisten her lower lip as she spoke.

'There I was thinking that I had piqued your interest from the moment you first laid eyes on me.'

Her cheeks became slightly pink and she redirected her gaze away from him. He felt his long-ignored libido spark to life, begging for satisfaction, but he kept it caged. He had made a promise that he would not pursue her. She had to come to him.

He sat back in his seat, stretching his arms above his head languorously. 'You insist that you're immune to my charms but you know that old saying—"the lady doth protest too much"...'

'It's a wonder this island has not sunk under the weight of your ego.'

'Careful, now, you don't want one of the locals to hear you talk like that.' He lowered his voice conspiratorially. 'There are many ancient ruins here, many old legends.'

She paled, frozen for a moment. 'Oh...of course. I didn't mean to...'

'The mermaids can get quite offended too.' He fought to maintain his facade but the sudden darkening of her expression had a rumble of laughter escaping his chest.

'Remind me never to take anything you say as truth.' She fought to hide her smile as she sipped her drink, eyes sparkling. 'I don't usually find it funny to be made sport of…but you are just so charming about it.'

'I don't see you as sport, Priya.' He met her eyes. 'Maybe I just challenged myself to make you laugh today. Nothing more.'

Her expression softened. 'No ulterior motives?'

He shook his head, knowing that it was the truth. He didn't see her as a game or distraction. Perhaps he never had. But that made his attraction to her even more complicated.

'If you no longer view me as a game to play, how do you see me?' she asked.

He considered his words for a long moment. 'I see you as something very rare, born into a world where so much is the same. You walked away from everything. You forged a new path and then you voluntarily chose to walk back into the fire to save people. You chose to marry me for completely selfless reasons and that is a badge that I cannot claim for myself. It's heroic.'

'Not just a vapid princess, then?'

'You hide your steel well, princess. But beneath all the beauty and polish lies a warrior.'

'A knight in a white wedding gown.' She smirked, twirling her finger around the rim of her glass slowly. 'I don't think you are quite as villainous as you try to behave. Perhaps we should just agree that we rescued one other and come to a truce.'

He opened his mouth to reply with something charming and flirtatious, as was his norm, but found he had no response. He was entranced by the softness of her lips and the warmth in her eyes. For once, he was not trying to manipulate her or charm her or any of the usual reasons that he conversed with people. Had she seen under his facade just as clearly as he had seen under hers?

He grew pensive, unconsciously letting an awkward silence fall over them. Suddenly the mood between them seemed stilted and tense, as though they were both stopping themselves from saying any more, from treading any further into the dangerous waters which they had entered.

Their food began to arrive and, sure enough, Dimitri had outdone himself with a platter of traditional souvlaki and fresh fish that would rival that of any five-star restaurant he had encountered.

He had not been lying to her when he'd said he treasured the small village just as much as he did one of his resorts. He had even asked Dimitri to come and work for him during the off season. The man had refused, stubbornly sticking to his small-town life. Not that Eros would blame him. Halki was a tiny slice of paradise. It had somehow remained immune to the chaotic hustle and bustle of the hectic tourism that had engulfed the rest of the islands around them. But that also left the people of Halki at more risk of unemployment and poverty.

His plans to nourish and build a sustainable tourism plan for these smaller islands in Greece was a clever one. Sure, it had begun as a way for him to help hard-working men like Dimitri, but ultimately it served his purposes too. It built his own personal wealth and furthered his status as a powerful investor and developer.

Just because he had a conscience it did not mean that he was a good person. He had stolen another man's bride for revenge and he planned to take and destroy his birth father's legacy without a thought for those who relied upon it. He was not a good man.

He watched as she groaned, biting into her swordfish and took another sip of her wine. The stress and tension of the previous week seemed to melt away from her slim shoulders and, in turn, he felt himself relax.

He had not anticipated this intense attraction… or whatever it was, and he had not anticipated liking this pampered society ice queen. As far as complications went, this one was new for him.

He thought of the call he had received from his team in New York the day before to tell him that his mother had been seen meeting with Vikram Davidson Khan. Arista was a powerful legal force in the financial world but even she couldn't damage the plan he'd put in place for Priya to take control of her family business.

Still, he couldn't shake off the feeling that he had pulled the wreckage of Priya's family company from the murky waters of bankruptcy only to paint a bright red target on them. But it was pointless to worry Priya about such a vague piece of information when there was nothing that she could do. She worked herself to the bone and deserved some time to unwind before the deal was finalised and they were thrown back into reality.

Priya noticed the change in Eros as they finished up their food and he moved to the kitchen at the back to thank the chef. As the men spoke in rapid Greek, she ambled along the wall of photographs and found a teenage Eros pictured in many of them, along with an older man who must be his stepfather. Stavros smiled broadly in each photo, not betraying any of the pain Eros had spoken of.

A computer sat on a table near the entrance and Priya noticed it was open on an internet search page. She turned her head to see if Eros was still deep in conversation, wondering if perhaps this was a test to see if she was trustworthy.

She bit her bottom lip. She could email Aria… but to what end?

Surprisingly she realised that she had no real urge to contact anyone. Technically, she was unemployed for the first time in seven years and although she was about to step into the biggest position of her career to date, for now she had no obligations. No one waiting for her, no one needing her to keep things together.

She found she was looking forward to perhaps spending a day on the beach tomorrow and reading rather than busying herself around the house as she had done for the past few days. The thought shocked her.

Eros appeared by her side without warning and she jumped. He looked down at the open computer and raised one brow.

'Apparently, unlike your island, Halki is a part of the twenty-first century.' She smiled crookedly. 'I didn't use it, if that's what you're thinking.'

'Do you want to?' he asked.

She crossed her arms over her chest. 'What about our rules?'

'I trust you.' He shrugged. 'I'm going to go run

a few errands around town, you can come with me or you can explore by yourself.'

She watched him walk away, feeling something warm and indescribable blooming in her chest at his words. What was happening between them? She had enjoyed his company so much the hours had flown by. She chose to stay with the computer for a moment, just to check her messages and send Aria a quick email to let her friend know that she was fine.

The lure of freedom to explore the picturesque seaside paradise was too much to ignore and she happily spent an hour wandering along the streets and drinking it all in. She had once dreamt of travelling the world at her leisure. She had once been carefree and full of hope for her future. Her work and her ambition drove her... but was that enough? She had existed for so long in an endless pursuit of scaling the ladders of power and seeking justice for her father's hard-won legacy...

When she looped back around to the harbour, Eros stood leaning against one of the pillars looking painfully handsome as usual. She felt her breath catch as he caught her eye and let a half-smile touch his lips.

'Dimitri has just told me that there is an evening of food and dancing planned later in the town square,' he said, extending his arm to her.

'Dancing,' Priya said with mock horror. 'Oh, no, you do not want to see me dance.'

He cocked his head to one side, those cerulean eyes sparkling with mischief. 'Well, now, I quite find that I do, as a matter a fact. As your travel guide, I insist.'

'Don't we need to keep a low profile?' She bit her bottom lip, feeling the insane pull to nestle closer into his side and drink in his strength. He was not hers, she reminded herself.

'I consider Halki more my home than anywhere else I've lived.' He shrugged. 'The Theodorou family were some of the first settlers. I was thinking we could stay the night and do some more exploring tomorrow. Keep that brain of yours occupied.'

The little farmhouse Eros had spoken of owning turned out to be a magnificently restored villa and old barn with original stonework that was joined perfectly by a glass wing with perfect views down over the cliffs. She was thankful that he had advised her to bring a change of clothing, and took the opportunity to shower and dress in an olive-green jersey sundress. She surveyed herself in the mirror and felt a wave of self-consciousness wash over her.

What would his community think, seeing someone so plain on Eros Theodorou's arm? She had no make-up with her, no jewellery or hair-styling products to accentuate what she knew was an entirely forgettable face.

But when she stepped out into the courtyard of the farmhouse and was instantly pinned by his appreciative gaze, she felt a dangerous ember of hope begin to glow within her.

She took his hand and tried to ignore the delicious scent of him as they strolled down the cobbled streets towards the small town square. Evidently some kind of festival was being celebrated because the square had been lit up with rings of small lanterns and lights strung between the buildings. People stopped Eros at every turn, kissing his cheeks and engaging in animated conversations she couldn't understand.

When one person congratulated them on their marriage, Priya darted her gaze to Eros, who quickly explained that Dimitri hadn't understood it was confidential and had already spread the joyful news around the island.

She looked around, seeing all the curious eyes on her. A strange feeling settled in her gut as he took her hand once more and led her into the centre of the crowd. A band had set up in the middle on a raised platform and a makeshift dance floor was filled with locals dancing gleefully in the fading evening light.

The day had passed so quickly, she realised.

A handful of stars were already beginning to appear.

'If you don't want to dance, I won't force you.' He led her to a low table and chairs at the edge of the dance floor. 'Sit here. I'll get us a drink.'

She watched him walk away and felt a weight settle in her chest. She would bet that a passionate man like him knew just how to move. She would bet that the women he usually dated were fabulous swan-like creatures who allowed him to swirl them around the dance floor in scandalously sensual positions. Unfortunately for both of them, she had absolutely no rhythm in her body and two clumsy left feet.

An older gentleman caught her eye and began moving towards where she stood motionless at the side of the dance floor.

'Good evening,' he said in husky Greek. 'Are you seeking a dance partner?'

Priya froze, turning her head in search of Eros. She spied him standing at the bar, one brow cocked playfully as he watched her awkward interaction. A slight smile played upon his lips. Damn him.

He would expect her to say no, she realised. He would expect her to be her usual stay-safe self.

Before she even knew what she was doing she had turned back to the gentleman and placed her hand in his, mumbling a quick thank you in

Greek that she had learned from the phrase book she had bought at the airport.

The man was smartly dressed in a blue shirt and black tailored trousers, his shoes polished to a high shine. He was the epitome of respect as he kept one hand deliberately above her waistline and the other on her left shoulder.

She tried to focus on the quick shuffling dance and found herself genuinely enjoying it after an initially nervous start. She was painfully aware of Eros as he moved across the square and took a seat at the edge of the dance floor. Even from her moving position she could see the women around him stare, desire in their gazes. He was pure alpha male, spreading out his legs and sipping his drink as he watched her.

'An old man like me should not make your husband jealous,' the man whispered in perfect English in her ear. 'But he watches you like he fears I will steal you away.'

'No…he doesn't care what I do,' she said quickly. The music ended and Priya took a step back, smiling tightly.

The old man smiled, taking a step back as well and looking at a spot just over her left shoulder. 'I think we have tested him enough with this dance meant for lovers.'

'I think so too.' Eros's voice came from behind her.

Priya turned, ready to chastise him, but Eros smoothly pulled her into his arms and began to guide them in a slow, seductive movement. As she had expected, he had almost professional dancing expertise and made her feel rather like a stuffed animal who was being pulled along in the dance rather than a participant.

'A dance for lovers,' he murmured near her ear. 'It is a pity that he has no idea that we are sworn enemies. Still, I thought I owed my bride a first dance.'

She tried to ignore the tightness of her breath in her chest and the tingles down her hips from where his hands made contact.

The material of her dress was too thin, the air was too hot, she could feel him everywhere, and the worst part was she did not want it to stop. For a woman who hated dancing, she could have moved around that dance floor with him all night. She felt feather-light in his arms and the way he moved was utterly magical. He made her feel like she *could* dance.

His hands tightened on her waist and she looked up to find him staring at a spot over her shoulder, his jaw set like steel.

'Did I do something wrong? I'm not really good at this,' she said quickly.

'Do you always assume that things are your fault?'

'It's okay, I know I'm terrible. I was given dance lessons as a teenager and even my dance partner abandoned me. Then the dance master kicked me out.' She laughed softly, remembering the horror on her mother's face when she had returned home just a week before her cotillion.

Before she could respond to him they were interrupted by the arrival of a beautiful redhead, a sultry smile on her lips as she reminded Eros that he had promised her a dance. Something dark twisted inside Priya's stomach.

'Is that okay?' Eros looked to her.

'Of course. By all means. I'm terrible at this anyway.' Priya avoided Eros's raised brows and the beautiful woman's sultry smile as she walked quickly back to the table he had recently vacated.

This entire day had become far too much. She was supposed to keep her distance from him. Now he was teaching her to fish, introducing her to his old friends and showing her his human side here on this beautiful island full of history. All of this had been so much easier when she had believed him to be an egotistical self-centred playboy, but it was becoming clear that there was far more beneath the surface than he chose to show.

She resisted looking back towards the dance floor for as long as she could manage. A part of her had wanted Eros to turn the redhead away, but he was known here. He was one of Halki's benefactors so of course he would dance and enjoy himself. Maybe he even knew the redhead already… The thought was jarring enough to give her the strength to look up, and what she saw made her stiffen with an emotion so dark and primal it made her shiver.

The beauty had coiled herself around Eros's body like a glove and he was gazing down at her with what she recognised to be one of his trade-mark charming smiles. He laughed at something the woman said, tipping his head back to the sky and revealing the strong column of his throat.

His hands were neutral, and there was nothing truly improper about the situation.

And he was free to dance with whoever he wanted, she reminded herself. Yes, the people here now knew that they were married but she and Eros still knew the truth of the matter. It was a business arrangement, a sham that should hold absolutely no effect on her feelings or actions. So then why was she struck by the dark urge to rush over and claim him as her own? Was she… jealous?

He wasn't hers. He couldn't be. He had only married her for revenge and once she had served her purpose he would discard her and dissolve their arrangement just as they'd agreed to. It wasn't personal…it couldn't be.

He'd made no secret of his attraction to her

and she'd done her best to ignore it but now, watching him flaunt his dancing skills with another woman in front of her, she wondered why on earth she had ever refused his offer. Why she had been so hell-bent on denying herself adventure in all its forms.

Eros Theodorou was the living embodiment of adventure and excitement and she was suddenly so, so sick of working so hard and letting life pass her by.

Before she knew what she was doing, she had stood and begun moving across the dance floor.

'Excuse me.' She arrived by their side and gently placed her hand on Eros's bicep. They stepped apart and Priya almost backed away as she felt the heat of his gaze on her. With a deep breath, she met his eyes, ignoring the presence of the other woman entirely.

'My husband has promised me the next dance.'

CHAPTER TEN

THE OTHER WOMAN'S eyes widened at her words and she meekly moved away into the crowd. Priya watched Eros's expression darken, his lips turning into a thin line. Was he angered by her obvious display of possession over him? She couldn't deny that's what it was. She could still feel the hum of adrenaline in her veins from fighting the urge to tear him away from the dance floor. What had come over her? She felt like she was losing all control.

Eros didn't speak, he simply extended his hand towards her and pulled her into the circle of his arms. The music sped up slightly and Priya felt the change in him. His hands were tight on her hips as they moved, urgent and possessive. True to her word, she had terrible rhythm, but somehow he seemed to smooth out her movements when she second-guessed herself. His confidence was infectious, as was his natural rhythm, and she found herself following him, allowing him to lead. It was a revelation.

Had she always been attempting to lead the dance in the past? Had that always been the problem? Or maybe she'd just never had a dance partner as skilled at taking control.

She felt warm and flustered and wild and she suddenly regretted following him onto this dance floor. She had never felt such a distinct pull of temptation for any man in the past. Keeping her precious control intact had always been of far greater worth to her than any other benefit. But in Eros Theodorou's arms she questioned everything.

He made her feel small and delicate and feminine and the worst part was that she liked it. He made her want to stop fighting and simply relax into his strength for a moment and it absolutely terrified her. She looked up to find his eyes on hers, serious and questioning.

His hands moved a fraction lower on her back, the heat of his fingertips like a brand. 'You didn't like watching me dance with her?'

'I decided that the only person who should be allowed to touch my husband is me.' She spoke the words on a rush of breath. Fear and longing and confusion were all seeming to amalgamate into adrenaline. She paused, moving closer to his ear. 'Maybe it's all just a part of the act. Or... maybe I am a spoilt princess after all.'

He moved her over his arm, dipping her backwards inch by inch as the music came to a crescendo. 'Is it bad that I find this possessive streak intensely seductive?'

'I'm not possessive.'

'Oh, you are.' Using one finger to hook her hair behind her ear, he trailed his thumb softly along her collarbone. 'It's possibly the one area in which we are not polar opposites. I've been staring down every man who looked your way since we arrived.'

She shivered under his touch, hating herself and loving it all at once. Was this always how it would be with him? Would she always feel this push and pull between good and bad, wrong and right?

He was the perfect temptation, and he was everything that she should never have or want for herself. He was dangerous. She had built her life around her safe, secure path to her goals. Eros was a walking hazard sign so why was she tempted to dive off the cliff?

'If you could hear my thoughts right now you would run.' His eyes had darkened to a storm, his fingers weaving a path up her ribcage. 'You should run.'

'Tell me.'

'I want to devour you right here on this dance floor.' His lips touched her ear as he continued to lead her in the dance's slow and seductive

rhythm. 'I want to see just how far I could push
you. How close I could get you to climax before
anyone around us would notice.'

'You once promised to ruin me.'

'You have been a good girl for far too long.
Even that first day in the limo I could sense the
real you hiding under all that ice, desperate for
release.'

The last word was little more than a whisper
in her ear. How could one word be filled with
such sinful promise?

She was so tired of being a good girl. She was
so tired of playing it safe and making plans and
always, *always* doing the right thing. Was he
right? Had she simply buried this part of herself
under her icy facade? She'd never thought of herself as sensual or passionate or any of the other
words he'd used to describe her in their verbal
sparring. And yet, when their bodies were close,
she felt it. She stopped holding back, consciously
leaning into the fire that had been steadily building within her since they'd begun dancing.

She leaned in and pressed her lips to his, soft
and tentative. He tasted like the sweetest sugar
mixed with the hard bite of liquor. A sensual
contradiction, just like the man himself.

As she deepened the kiss, he seemed to growl
underneath her lips and tongue. He gave her a
moment to take the lead, standing still and be-

coming pliant under her touch. Holding her as she devoured him, feeling whatever control she had left melt away in the heat of their embrace.

This was what she had felt, she realised. This was what had been taunting her, building tension within her at every tense interaction they'd had over the past week. Her body had craved this man so deeply it had consumed her, even if her mind had refused to acknowledge it. As if he sensed her losing control, he tightened his hold on her waist, easing her with gentle strokes of his hands along her nape.

He broke the kiss, pulling back a few inches, and she practically growled at him to come back.

'There she is,' he purred, trailing one hand down the side of her neck and pressing lightly. 'Tell me…do you know what you want yet?'

'I want you to take me somewhere…' She felt the hitch in her breath, felt his gaze scorching her with its intensity. 'I want to explore this… whatever this madness is. Then maybe we can get back to our lives.'

'You want this to be over before I've even begun?' His fingers trailed along her collarbone and down the side of her breast. 'If you think you can keep a lid on this tightly coiled control while you're in my bed, you are very mistaken.'

Her lust-scrambled brain struggled to process his words until they began to move to the music once more and she felt his thigh press between her legs. His eyes were filled with dark promise as he moved against her and to her shock and awe she felt herself moisten.

She tried to relax, her eyes darting around to the other couples dancing, oblivious to the torrid scene in their midst. It was depraved, it was probably skirting the law...it was the most excited she had ever felt.

'What are you doing?' She breathed heavily.

'Giving you a taste of what's to come,' he murmured in her ear.

She dug her nails into his bicep, stifling the moan that wished to burst free from her lips. It was torture, delicious, sensual torture. She closed her eyes as the pressure between her legs intensified.

'Look at me, Priya. Tell me that you want this to be done quickly. Tell me that once will be enough. *Damn*, I can feel how close you are to the edge.'

She cursed under her breath and felt his chest vibrate on a growl. He was so male, surrounding her with his primal heat, and deep down she knew how dangerous it was to accept this offer. She could see now why others had never wanted it to end. He was a force of addictive sensual energy and even the sight of him dancing with another woman had got her claws out.

Who had she become?

She didn't care that there were people nearby, she didn't care about anything but holding him closer while he worked his magic, grinding the pleasure higher and higher...

'That's enough, I think.' Eros stepped away, staring down at her with a look on his face that was pure male possession. 'The first climax I give you will be for my eyes only.'

'Yes. I want that very much.' She gasped, hardly believing the words that came from her own lips. He couldn't either, judging by the stunned expression on his face. His lips were a deep swollen red from her kisses, and she shivered as they curved into a sinful smile. Taking her by the hand, he practically pulled them from the square at speed, barely pausing to wave goodnight to Dimitri.

Eros carried Priya up the pathway to his farmhouse, the only place he'd truly felt happiness, and was suddenly intensely grateful that he'd thought to stock up on protection. He'd never brought another woman here in all the years he'd owned it, but today, with Priya, he'd wanted to be prepared just in case. No matter what reputation he had on the mainland, he was not the type to use and discard women at will. He needed to feel an attraction, a sense of connection. But he had never felt anything like this.

When he looked down at the woman in his arms she beamed up at him, her face flushed from their frantic rush back from town. The feeling that had plagued him all day seemed to pulse within his chest, making him claim her mouth in another brutal kiss. The last shred of resistance within him broke completely, threatening to unleash the wildness he had been keeping locked down. But he needed to know that she wanted this too, that she wanted him and not just what he could give her.

'This has never been a game for me, Priya. Despite what you might think, I'm not the kind of man who flirts with everything with a pulse.'

'What makes me the exception?'

'I don't quite know,' he said, surprising himself with his own honesty. 'All I know is that from the moment I first laid eyes on you I have craved this. I have become rather addicted to your scent and the way you move and I want nothing more than to take you into my bed and not let you free until we are both thoroughly satisfied. But if you say no… I will walk away.'

'I don't want to say no.' She breathed deeply, stepping closer.

'Thank God for that.' He reached out, running a finger from her wrist up to the tip of her shoulder blade and feeling her shiver under his touch. 'I think it would have killed me.'

She undulated under his touch, reaching out to lay her hands flat against his chest. 'You make me not care about the rules so much and that is a dangerous quality in a man.'

'I'm a dangerous man, Priya. But not to you. Never to you.'

Without another word, he closed the gap between their lips and felt her meet him halfway. Her hands were all over him, touching and burrowing into his unbound hair as though she had been craving it. He heard the low groan in the back of her throat and thought he might come on the spot at the delicious sounds she made.

He lifted her against him, moving faster than he'd have thought possible as she laughed against his lips. The whitewashed walls and modest comfortable furniture of the living area passed in a blur as he guided them both down the hall to the master bedroom.

The sensation of her teeth scraping the bottom edge of his neck was almost enough to make him lose control entirely. *Take it slow*, he reminded himself. Something told him that she was easily spooked. For such a confident woman she seemed almost afraid of her own sexuality. She was a delicious puzzle that he felt compelled to solve, even when he knew that this was a temporary entanglement. A short-term release from the pressures of reality.

But somehow, knowing that she felt the same, hadn't given him the reassurance he'd expected. For a man who had experienced the obsessions of former partners, finding the one woman who didn't want more from him should be akin to stumbling upon heaven itself.

He ignored the thought, stroking upward along the soft, bare skin at the back of her sundress, pulling the material down at her shoulders. Priya laughed at his urgency but once her eyes landed on the impressive antique four-poster bed, she visibly froze for a moment.

'Everything okay?' he asked, fully prepared to stop.

She nodded a little too quickly, reaching up to continue his slow undressing herself. The dress was pulled down more, revealing a lacy white bra. Eros was silent as he teased one fingertip along the rim of the lace, watching as her skin turned to gooseflesh and she shivered. Priya kept her eyes closed, her breathing ragged as she undid the clasp and slowly bared herself to him. Reverently, he took both sizeable breasts in his hands.

Finally, something within him growled. Not wasting a single moment, he kept his eyes on hers as he ran his tongue along one tip.

She hissed between her teeth at the contact and then groaned, grinding her pelvis against his.

'You like that,' he murmured against her breast, using his other hand on its twin. 'You like just that little hint of hardness with the soft.'

'I don't really know what I like but I like that.'

Her words stuck in his mind for a moment as he wondered how she could not know what she liked. The thought that she'd had selfish lovers in the past infuriated him. He continued kissing and teasing the hard peak of her breast, loving each tiny sound of pleasure that escaped her lips. Every new touch and response made him want to spend hours finding out where she was most sensitive.

He stood back up to his full height, pulling her closer and claiming her lips once more. She surprised him by sliding her hands down his back and exploring his muscles.

But when he lowered his hands to her hips and slid them even lower she froze.

'Wait.'

That single word was all it took. He stepped back, sliding his arms away from her body even as everything within him growled in protest.

Her face was drawn with tension as she struggled with some internal debate. Finally, she spoke. 'I know a little of your experience, mainly that you've had quite a lot of it.'

'I don't need you to tell me how many partners you've had, Priya, that's your business.' He ran his hand down the soft skin of her arm, reluctant to break any contact between them. 'I'm here with you, not your number.'

'What if the number directly related to my... experience?' She stiffened in his arms, pulling away and turning to face out towards the sea. 'My first engagement left scars that I never quite managed to shake off. I had dated guys before Eric, I had enjoyed male attention but after... I questioned every man who showed interest in me. I questioned everybody, even friends. I isolated myself from everyone except Aria.'

He waited for her to elaborate but she seemed to visibly shrink from his gaze. He coiled a tight leash around his frustrated libido and placed his arms firmly on her shoulders, stopping the exit he knew she was poised for. Holding her in the moment before she retreated.

He would not judge her inexperience, just as he would not judge her for the opposite if that were true, but still his brain struggled to process what her words meant.

She practically exuded sexuality in the way she walked, in the way she spoke, even in the delicate way she ate her food. She was all contradictions. Just when he thought he had her worked out, she revealed another layer.

'I was young, I had this foolish notion of saving such a special moment for my wedding night and then…well, you know how that went. Afterwards, I told myself that I didn't need to date or have sex to live a fulfilling life and I don't.' She turned to face him, her lips in a hard line. 'For the most part, I've effortlessly ignored my virginity…until I met you.'

CHAPTER ELEVEN

FOR A LONG moment the only sound was the wind coming in through the tiny sapphire-blue window. Priya felt the tension in her jaw as she forced herself to remain still, to keep her feet planted and resist the urge to walk away from this conversation and the intense look in Eros's eyes as he ran a hand through his long blond hair.

'With your track record in the boardroom I'm not surprised that you've had no time for men.' The barest hint of a smile touched his firm lips. 'I'd be lying if I said I wasn't extremely turned on at being the first to tempt you.'

'I thought you were the kind of man who would be absolutely horrified at the idea he had been courting a real-life virgin.'

'As opposed to an imaginary one?'

She let out a sound that was half breath, half laugh, and closed her eyes tightly, words completely failing her. She always knew what to say, always knew how to talk herself out of every situation, but something about this beautiful infuriating man seemed to short-circuit every one of the synapses in her brain.

She felt the warmth of him even though he still did not touch her. She opened her eyes and was met with a look of dark desire.

'You may be inexperienced but you are still one of the most sensual women I've ever met. If you honestly think this changes anything for me…' He bit his lower lip, moving closer and gripping her chin gently. 'I have never wanted a woman more than you.'

She felt the tension in her body thrum when she saw the heat in his gaze. She'd expected a different reaction to her disclosure. She'd expected him to retreat, for his interest to wane. It was only now she realised how relieved she was that it hadn't.

Almost on reflex, she felt her body lean into his and heard the harsh exhalation of his breath as his lips pressed into the sensitive skin of her neck.

'I want you too,' she said quietly, leaning back to meet his eyes. 'I want you to be my first, Eros.'

Their kiss was a harsh meeting of lips and tongue, the frantic need that had been building and doused over and over now finally roaring to a blaze. Feeling emboldened by her own admission, Priya moved backwards until she was lying on the bed. He was on her in an instant, his lips trailing fire along her skin. But when he finally moved his fingertips between her legs and she tensed, he paused, the first look of uncertainty she had ever seen on his face.

'Before I told you the truth about myself, you promised to ruin me for all others.' She took his hand, slowly sliding it back to the spot he'd just vacated, hardly believing her own actions. 'I want all of you, Eros. Please don't hold back.'

After a few slow slides of his fingertips through her sensitive folds, he seemed to zero in on the most sensitive spot. Priya felt sparks of pleasure shoot up her spine and loosen all her muscles in a pleasurable warmth. He kept up a slow rhythm, all the while kissing her and whispering growls of encouragement in her ear. She could see in his eyes how much he was enjoying seeing her lose control and that realisation made her give in to him more and more with every new wave of pleasure.

When he slid one finger deep inside her she bit down on her lip so hard she thought she tasted blood. Then he added a second and all coherent thought left her. Was it possible to die from too much pleasure? Her body seemed to convulse and shake with every thrust and she was shocked to recognise the throbbing tightening sensation of an imminent climax.

He seemed to know just how to bring her back down to earth with gentle kisses and kneading of his strong hands on her thighs. Then she was pulling his shoulders, guiding him to where she needed him most. Pleasure was a drug that had them both in its thrall.

After a moment of grappling with a foil packet, he moved above her and met her eyes. The connection was so intense; she almost spoke the crazy words that had been building within her all day. Intense, passionate feelings that she knew were too much for whatever this was between them. She pushed the thoughts away, focusing on the moment, on the feel of his strong hips between her widespread thighs and the sight of his golden hands pinning her waist as he slowly thrust inside her.

To her surprise, there was no pain, only a feeling of intense pleasure she had never known she craved. He was an expert lover, whispering deep murmurs of encouragement in her ear while simultaneously building the force of their rhythm to the one she craved most. She didn't want him to be gentle and he seemed to understand without her ever voicing the words. She worked her hips, matching him and taking him deeper with each brutal thrust. She could tell the moment that he began to lose control, as his biceps clenched and he let out a low curse that was part moan.

The sight of him becoming lost to this primal force between their bodies was enough to send the fire within her burning in an upward spiral once more.

'I think I'm going to…' She could barely speak with the intensity of sensation building inside her, it was almost too much and yet she couldn't quite…

'I'll get you there,' he growled, reaching under her hips and pulling her up at an angle. Somehow he found the exact spot that she needed and pressed down, sliding slow torturous circles over her sensitive flesh.

The combination of him moving inside her and his expert touch was like lighting a hidden fuse within her. She'd never once felt anything like the trembling ripples that overcame her as she succumbed to an earth-shattering climax. And in the same breath Eros was right there with her, growling her name as he buried his face in her hair.

Eros awoke to an empty bed.

He found her sitting out in the glass conservatory that overlooked the crashing waves of the bay, the moon bathing her silk-covered figure in silvery light. For a long moment he simply breathed in the sight of her sitting in his favourite wingback chair as though she belonged there.

When she looked up, he saw the guarded look in her eyes and felt his own uncertainty take hold. They hadn't discussed what their decision tonight might mean going forward.

It had been her first time and they'd made love three times in the night. He cursed himself for being so thoughtless. 'Are you sore?'

'No. I'm…' She shook her head, biting her lower lip.

'Tell me,' he urged.

'I had to leave that bed…because I woke up and you were lying beside me and I just wanted you all over again. Is it always like that?'

He had to fight not to lose control there and then. As she looked up at him and smiled with such shy innocence, he thought, *Mine*, with such force it knocked the breath from his chest.

Had it ever been like this for him before? Tomorrow they could deal with the aftermath of this madness. Here, now, he would give in to his own selfish need to possess her. He would claim her again and again, as no other man had.

But first… First, he would make her scream his name a few more times. He lowered himself down to kneel between her thighs, pressing her back against the chair with one hand.

She spread her legs, reaching for him, and he shook his head as he skimmed his fingertips down the insides of her thighs, baring her to him. She was all woman, the perfect tapestry of caramel perfection where the glow from the moon bathed her in shadows and light.

He traced the centre of her with one finger, watching her eyes flutter closed then open again, as though she couldn't quite decide if she could watch. He began a slow path of feather-light kisses at her knee, feeling her breath catch as he neared his inevitable destination.

She met his eyes, a shy smile on her swollen lips, and suddenly he felt something he hadn't encountered since his teens. Uncertainty. His past fell away…all the accolades of his bedroom prowess, all his own bravado.

He looked into Priya's eyes, poised above her most intimate flesh, and he swallowed past the lump in his throat.

'I want to devour you.' His voice was a thin rasp in the silence. 'And I want you to watch me.'

Her breath shuddered in her chest as she nodded once and he gripped her thighs, pushing them wide. The woman seemed to set him on fire. He pressed his lips against perfect folds and felt her hips rise as though answering the motion. Such a fast learner, his little wife. He hummed his approval against her folds and heard her let out a very unladylike curse of pure pleasure.

'More,' she gasped, her fingers tentatively touching the hair that had fallen across his face.

Touching it like perhaps she wanted to take hold and command just how much more she would like.

The image snapped his control completely, igniting the embers of his endless hunger.

Like a man starved, he commenced his feast.

The next few days passed in a blur of lovemaking and hushed conversations.

They returned to the island to continue the work on the house together, spending the days toiling under the warm autumn sun and nights consumed by a different kind of heat. The dark stillness of the night paved the way for intimate conversations Priya had never believed herself capable of. She told him about the anxiety that had always been a part of her and he shared flashes of his own difficult upbringing, revealing a vulnerability she would have never guessed at.

When the subject of her first engagement came up, she didn't brush it off as she usually did. She shared in detail the terrible deceit and pressure to marrry that had led to her running away from society. He was furious but didn't prod when she changed the subject.

She didn't feel the need to pretend around him, she didn't worry that he would take advantage of her for showing weakness, and perhaps that was the most dangerous thing of all about this illicit affair they had embarked upon.

Her joy bloomed into a weightless happiness as he continued to show her slices of adventure each day, along with unbelievable pleasure. Priya knew that she should be cautious. She knew that nothing good could come from taking this man's hand and following blindly to whatever new slice of heaven he offered.

But when she was with him…it felt good. More than that, *she* felt good. As if with every kiss and touch he was wiping away some of the darkness inside her and letting some of his glowing vitality shine in.

It won't last, that voice within whispered.

The voice was particularly strong one afternoon after she overheard Eros on the satellite phone to his legal team. He seemed agitated, pacing the floor of the villa like a caged animal. When he saw her watching him, he quickly ended the call.

'Is everything okay?' she asked, dreading the answer.

'We need to return to New York sooner than I had planned.'

'Is there a problem with the deal?' She crossed her hands over her chest and felt the simple action shift something between them. A shutter seemed to come down over Eros's eyes as he took in her anxious pose. They hadn't mentioned their arrangement once in the week since they'd first made love. It was as though they'd entered an unspoken truce.

'My mother has decided to take an interest in the proceedings. It's just best that I'm there in person while things are finalised.'

Priya nodded at his vague answer, feeling a barrage of confusing emotions threaten to overwhelm her. When his phone rang once more, she was grateful for the interruption and slipped back to her bedroom to pack her things.

How had it only been a couple of weeks since she'd come to this slow-paced slice of tranquillity?

The sun was beginning to set on the waves below, casting an orange glow over the white stone walls of the villa. She stepped out onto the balcony, breathing in the scent of bougainvillea and salt that had somehow become a balm to her soul. Eros had been right, she'd been so wound up and in need of a little adventure in her life. If that was the only positive thing she took from this time here, maybe it would be enough.

Their flight back to the mainland was quick and soon they were seated on a private charter flight out of Athens, the orange glowing lights of the city disappearing in the distance below

them. Priya had felt the distance growing between them from the moment they'd left the island, neither of them wanting to be the one to
speak first and say what needed to be said.

She sensed him before she saw him from the
corner of her eye taking a seat across from her.
'You seem lost in thought.'

'I'm feeling grateful for the past couple of
weeks, that's all,' she said. "Now that it's over,
I feel like I should thank you for showing me
such a perfect slice of paradise.'

He froze, the strangest mixture of anger and
disbelief on his face. 'Thank you?'

His expression was dark and unreadable as
he stared out the window, into the distance. 'Are
we talking about the island or about the sex? Do
you plan to leave me a star rating somewhere?
Maybe check me off on one of your lists in your
planner?'

'That's not fair, Eros.' She frowned, confused
and hurt at his cruelty. 'I'm trying to be logical
about this.'

'Logic? That's what you want?' he asked softly.

'It's the path of least risk, isn't it?' She
shrugged, not knowing how the conversation
had got so tense. 'We both know we've been
stupid, letting this affair go on without any rules
in place.'

'I told you, I don't play by the rules,' he growled.

'Well that's one of the many reasons why we are incompatible.' She realised she was breathing hard and turned away from him with frustration. 'Because I do. I need them. I have a plan for what I need to achieve and—'

'I'm not a part of the plan. Got it.' He laughed, a low hollow sound. 'Well, you weren't a part of my plan either and yet here we are.'

A long moment passed between them. She had never seen him this way, all his bravado and charm stripped away. He seemed angry. At her.

Could it be that he wanted more?

Uncertainty kept her frozen in place. The prolonged silence was frigid and unbearable after the scorching inferno of the past week.

'I don't trust myself, Eros,' she whispered. 'If we don't draw the line now, when will it be the right time? I'm not practised in these kinds of arrangements. Especially not when the man in question is already my husband.'

'I know you're right,' he said gruffly. 'But I can't get enough of you.'

'Should I be flattered?' She attempted humour but the words that escaped her lips was tempered by fear. She was tempted by the thought of more time with Eros, but the logical side of her she had buried away was beginning to resurface. Deep down, she knew this was a terrible idea.

'You should be afraid,' he growled next to her

ear, gently nipping at the skin and soothing it with his devilish tongue. 'I have no control when it comes to you. None.'

For a long moment all she could feel was his heat against her, his arms anchoring her body ever tighter to fit against him as he wrought sensual torture down her neck. The sensation of being his sole focus was intense, as he'd told her it would be. But the thought that this was all some practised act was suddenly unbearable to her.

'Is this real?' she asked on a whisper of breath. 'Why is this suddenly so different for you? Why me?'

For a moment she thought she had ruined everything. That he might turn away from her and choose to finally end whatever madness they were courting. Instead, he pressed his forehead to hers and let out a long exhalation. 'Priya... I'm not the kind of man who makes promises outside the boardroom.'

'I don't want you to,' she said quickly, knowing she wasn't being entirely truthful. But even if he did decide he wanted more than just a fling, what kind of future could they have?

His lips claimed hers in a searing kiss that took her breath away. He was all around her, consuming her, and she felt like she could have burnt for all eternity with the ferocity of the pas-

sion that rose within her. She had thought that
this might have ebbed now that they'd spent the
past two weeks together. But it seemed the opposite was true. The more she was with him,
the more she wanted to be with him. The more
he touched her, the more she craved his touch.

Suddenly the thought that she might walk
away from this marriage unscathed was utterly
ridiculous. He had once jokingly promised to
ruin her for all other men... Right now, with his
lips tracing a fiery path between her breasts and
lower, she worried that he was right, and that he
might have left his imprint on her for ever. That
she would never stop measuring every other sexual experience she might have to this one. She
would never be free of the ghost of this wonderful, perfect pleasure that he stirred up within her.

But it wasn't just the pleasure she was addicted
to, it was him. It was his playful nature and the
passion he put into all his endeavours. The freedom with which he shared his thoughts. He was
her opposite yet in so many ways they were one
and the same.

She closed her eyes, feeling emotion threaten
at the back of her eyelids, and prayed that she
would keep her composure. Focus on the pleasure, she told herself. Focus on the present.

But then he growled, lifting her up and putting
her legs around his waist and began telling her

all the beautiful things he thought about her as he walked them towards the bedroom to the rear of the plane. When he laid her down on the bed and rose over her, his blue eyes glowing in his perfect face, she thought of the fact that eventually this would come to an end and felt something freeze inside her. Closing her eyes, she pushed away the uncomfortable emotions and allowed herself to be swept away into passion.

CHAPTER TWELVE

EROS TOOK ONE last look at Priya's sleeping form in the dawn light of his penthouse. He had kept her awake half of the night and it was only fair that he let her sleep, even if he was sorely tempted to wake her up for one last kiss before he went to his meeting.

When he finally emerged out into the cool morning air of the city he opted to walk, feeling a sense of calm.

From the first moment they'd met, he'd known that she was a woman who prided herself on control. Perhaps in the beginning he had seen her as a challenge, a fortress to be breached and conquered to prove his own prowess. Or perhaps he had simply told himself that over and over to avoid investigating this deep connection between them any further.

Maybe it was some outdated male instinct that came from seeing his ring on her finger or maybe it was the fact that she'd told him she trusted him.

Maybe he enjoyed her fiery wit and her open dislike of his public persona. Who knew what it was? All he knew was that he had never wanted a woman more…

She had said she didn't want to use him for sex, but he was used to being used. There was comfort in knowing where the intimacy began and ended. No games, no emotional entanglements or pain. There couldn't be a more ideal situation for two people who prized their own space. He would give her exactly what she wanted. He would show her the depths of that intense sensuality that he could feel hidden deep inside her.

He wasn't ready for this to be over just yet.

He had decided to allow his mother to name the terms of their meeting. It simply wasn't worth it to squabble over the details, not when there was so much at stake.

Eros arrived at the tall glass building that had housed Mytikas Holdings for decades, the realm of Zeus. Their investment banking headquarters spanned the top four floors of the shining tower at the centre of the financial district, and here was where Zeus had truly been treated as a god amongst men, using fear and intimidation to rule.

As the lift rose to the top floor, Eros felt the eyes of men and women on him. Though the sun had barely risen in the sky, the offices were already teeming with people. There was a reason why the Mytikas name was at the top of the chain. There had been newspaper articles documenting the hellish landscape that interns encountered here, the legacy of overworked employees and unequal opportunities. But unlike Davidson Khan, Mytikas Holdings had never been bankrupted despite countless lawsuits and accusations of exploitation.

But as he walked along the thickly carpeted halls of the open-plan office space, he was surprised to find people drinking coffee and talking at volume. The top floor looked almost... normal. These people did not look unhappy or overworked.

Priya's words came back to him, her confession that she worried over the staff employed in her father's company. For the first time he wondered what would happen to all these people once he dismantled Mytikas. He couldn't employ them all in his own company. What about the families that relied on them?

Even as the thought entered his head he pushed it away. He was not being selfish. He had waited for over a decade for this revenge, ever since Zeus had sent him away. There had once been a time when he'd dreamed of running this building as his father's right-hand man. A dream that had been taken from him.

He was shown to one of the large boardrooms

that overlooked the city but there was no sign of his older brother sitting at the head of the marble conference desk. Instead, his mother entered the room alone through the door at the opposite end of the room.

Arista strode into the room with her usual confidence, leaning one hip against the tabletop as she levelled him with a look of pure disdain.

'Lovely to see you, darling. I hear congratulations are in order. You didn't think to tell your own mother about your plans?'

This close, he could see that fine lines had finally begun to appear around her eyes and the perpetually youthful glow she exhibited had begun to dim. She was still beautiful but she suddenly looked her age. Above all…she looked miserable. For the first time he actually believed that the death of her long-time lover had truly had an effect on her. That it wasn't just an act. She looked like a woman in mourning.

'I couldn't risk you double-crossing me,' he shrugged, refusing to feel any pity for this woman who only ever seemed to cause him pain. 'Where is Xander? I want to see his face when he realises he's set to lose everything.'

'He's on his honeymoon,' Arista said in a flat tone. 'But he was kind enough to fire me before he left.'

Eros fought to keep his expression neutral,

not wanting to give her one ounce of pity. Because that was the only reason she was here. She wanted to manipulate him. The fact that his brother was on his honeymoon meant absolutely nothing... Unless...somehow... Xander had managed to beat him to the altar. It was impossible. Wasn't it?

'When was the wedding?' he gritted through his teeth.

'The same day as yours. Almost to the minute.' Her face hardened, a look of distaste on her polished features.

'I will contest him in court. This—this means n-nothing.' He froze at the familiar sense of his mouth moving slower than his thoughts. He felt pain in his jaw from gritting his teeth, the effort of controlling his mouth. Of keeping his stutter from resurfacing in his mother's presence. His mother narrowed her eyes for a moment but didn't comment.

'You have an important choice to make now, son.'

Her use of the word *son* jarred him, and for a moment he thought she looked almost remorseful. He shook off the sentiment. 'I will contest him. I won't stop until this company is in the dust.'

'I'm tired of these games, Eros. I'm tired of this life, aren't you?' Arista said, a frown pulling her mouth downward as she turned her face to look out at the clouds moving in over the city. Another thunderstorm, no doubt.

'It was never going to be yours, Mother.' Eros surprised himself by speaking the words with relative softness. 'Zeus was never going to see you as his equal. The man was a chauvinist as well as a control freak.'

'You cannot choose who you fall for, Eros.' Arista stood up to her full six-foot height once more, pulling a pristine white handkerchief from a hidden pocket in her skirt. 'Despite his myriad faults, we loved each other…and I believe that he loved you too, in his own way.'

Eros laughed, a sound so sharp and devoid of warmth he saw his mother flinch.

'Your dealings with your brothers and the inheritance clause are between the three of you now. I'm sorry I ever got involved.' She shook her head softly. 'But once I knew you had married the Davidson Khan heiress, I began digging…'

His mother watched him for a moment before shaking her head sadly and sliding a slim folder across the marble table. Eros scanned the contents and felt his stomach drop, his heart thumping in his chest as he realised what his mother had done. 'Why? She didn't deserve to be dragged into our war this way.'

'Believe me or not, but I did this to protect you. To stop you from being ruined by association. You've built so much for yourself.'

'She has waited for this for years,' he growled. 'It was my job to protect her.'

'I've never seen you this way. Eros…do you love this woman?' Arista's eyes gleamed with an uncharacteristic show of emotion.

The question jarred him, making him feel the same cloying madness he'd felt on the plane when Priya had said they needed to end things. It was an infatuation, he told himself. Nothing more.

He stood up, turning away from his mother's knowing gaze. This change in her was far more discomfiting than anything her old calculating self had done. He needed to think, to try to figure out a way out of this tangled mess where he was forced to choose between his own desire for revenge or Priya's entire future.

He could walk away from revenge or he could walk away from her.

She had never been meant to factor into his plan at all. She had simply been a pawn to use for his own aims. When exactly had she become more? At what point had she come to influence his decisions? When had she begun to matter so much to him?

Looking at that folder filled him with such

rage it was as though someone had directly threatened him. She was his wife so perhaps he could fool himself by saying he feared for her reputation, being associated with such boundless corruption. She would still have her inheritance to do with as she wished.

But suddenly his plans for revenge seemed hollow when it came at such a cost. He did not wish to cause her pain. The terrible truth of it all was that he would rather go through the pain himself to avoid her having to endure it.

She had been poised to embark upon a new life, finally in control of the empire she had been born to run. She was a princess about to step into the role of queen. He tried to figure out a way through this that didn't involve risking her walking away from him for ever.

'Does anyone else know about this evidence?'

'You haven't heard the news yet?' Arista said quietly. A look that could almost pass for guilt crossed her face. 'I thought that was why you were here. It wasn't in my original plans. But I was legally obligated to forward what I found.'

'What did you do?' Eros growled, fear clutching at his chest.

'Her uncle was arrested last night and all assets seized. Davidson Khan is being shut down.'

Eros was already moving towards the door, mentally mapping the quickest journey across town to his penthouse before Priya found out. She couldn't be alone when she heard this news...she needed to hear his side first.

'I'm sorry, Eros.' His mother's words flew at his back but he kept moving, barely registering the uncharacteristic emotion in her voice as he focused on getting to his wife.

The elevator doors opened and Priya walked into the spacious, polished mahogany corridors of Davidson Khan Financial. She remembered being a small child and roaming these halls, chased by her father, his voice booming after her.

This place had been his home—that workaholic tendency had not come from nowhere. She smiled sadly to herself as she took in the small empire where her father had once been king.

The office was empty. Papers lay scattered on desks, chairs pushed back from half-opened drawers. It was like a scene from a disaster movie where people see the tornado coming through the windows and they just dropped their papers and ran.

The phone call from Sorelli, their family lawyer, had come an hour before.

Your uncle was arrested last night. Everything is gone.

It had taken a few minutes for his words to sink in as she'd lain frozen in the bed that still held Eros's warmth. The older man had calmly informed her that while she had been distracted in Greece, a pre-purchase investigation had been launched by Arcum Investments that had unearthed a vast array of secrets her uncle had been hiding. The resulting findings had been passed to the authorities and had now wrought irrevocable damage. If she tried to lay claim to the company as it sank, it would only take her own name down too.

She had rushed through the morning city traffic, panic and disbelief sending her heartbeat wild. There had to be a logical explanation for it all but when she had arrived at the office building she'd found that they had all left, every single one of them. So much for fighting for the people. Her heart sank as she walked down the centre aisle towards the executive suites at the end. The larger corner offices were usually where the higher-ups behind their desks made the big decisions that would impact everyone. She felt anger build within her as she neared the largest office of all. The place that was supposed to be hers.

Her birthright.

She eased down into the wingback chair that had once been her father's favourite spot to sit and think or bellow orders across the room. Could it all be true? Could he have been a part of such fraudulent acts? She thought of the countless secret meetings that had taken place at their home in the Hamptons, the late-night phone calls. Was it possible that she had seen only what she'd wanted to see? Her father may not have been perfect but she refused to believe he was a bad person. Surely he did not deserve to have his life's work erased?

She did not deserve it either. As she watched the busy New York streets below she found she had no energy for anger. All she felt was the crippling black hole of betrayal she had fallen into. It was so like that moment all those years ago. Another office, another time when she'd had her trust brutally shattered by someone she'd loved. Only this time she'd given herself to Eros willingly. Body and soul.

Of course she hadn't learned from her mistakes. Of course she had fallen in love with him, she realised with a pitiful sob. She had always laughed at people who claimed they had fallen in love at first sight, but she had been entranced with him from the beginning. Been pulled under his spell. Could it really be that he had been planning to find a way out of their bargain?

In the two weeks they had spent together on that island there had been countless moments when he could have mentioned his concerns about the firm. She was not so obsessed with becoming CEO that she would have ignored fraud at this level. She would have listened. But maybe this had been the point all along, a dark voice spoke from deep down. Maybe he had never intended to obey the terms of their deal. He liked to break and bend the rules to fit his own needs, he'd even said as much.

Something broke within her as she realised that all the evidence pointed to Eros's deception and the only hope she clung to was influenced by that foolish girl within her who just wanted to believe she hadn't been fooled again.

The realisation that she had only been out of the city for such a short time was startling. It had felt like another world. Could she be so utterly changed in such a short space of time? The old Priya would have run out of this place fuelled by anger and rage, ready to wreak revenge. But she felt deflated, as if with this final blow he had knocked all the fight out of her. She had let her guard down, she had left herself open for a breach of this nature. But she was so tired of fighting.

She had never been a coward in her life. She hadn't even truly run from her mother once she'd found out about her deception and had walked away from her first wedding. She had moved away to college when the time was right. If she'd been invited to an event she had attended with her head held high, always knowing that she would return and take back what was rightfully hers.

But the idea of ever seeing Eros again and having to face what he had done was more than she could bear.

She closed her eyes, praying that the tears would not come, praying that she could stand up and walk out of this room with her head held high. She had no idea what she was going to do. She had no idea who she was without the goal of continuing her father's legacy. She still had his money; it would become unlocked soon. But she had never wanted it. Perhaps, deep down, she had known it was not an entirely honest fortune.

She took the same elevator that she had taken two weeks before and emerged into the foyer, standing and staring at the spot where she had first laid eyes on Eros Theodorou.

I'm here to ruin you.

His words from that first day haunted her, their eerie prophecy more than she could bear. He had achieved his goal. She had never felt such destruction of her defences. It was only once she stood out on the pavement and felt the first rain-drops hit her head that she realised she had absolutely no idea where she was supposed to go. Not back to his penthouse anyway. He could keep her clothes, he could keep everything, she just...she wanted to be alone.

Her stomach dropped as a sleek black limo came powering up the street and stopped directly in front of her. *Not him. Not now,* she prayed silently.

But of course it was him.

He stepped out into the rain, all blue eyes and powerful grace. She didn't have to ask if he knew what had happened. She could see it in his face.

'Get into the car.' His voice was deep, filled with an emotion she couldn't quite name. It certainly wasn't guilt anyway. He had told her himself, he never felt shame for completing business.

'Go to hell.' She spoke the words on impulse and saw him flinch as though she'd hit him. He didn't respond immediately; she saw his throat work as he exhaled a long, slow breath.

'Priya...if you would just let me explain.'

'Did you start the investigation?' She shot the question at him, not giving him a chance to charm his way around his actions. She was done being lied to and manipulated by the men around her. 'Yes or no?'

'Yes, I started it.'

His admission struck her squarely in her chest and she looked away, praying that she could finish this and get away without losing her composure.

'It's standard practice at Arcum but then my mother got involved, intent on sabotaging our arrangement, and... I never intended it to go this way, I promise you.'

'Forgive me if your promises don't hold a lot of weight with me.' She steeled her jaw, needing to get away from him before she crumbled entirely. 'You see, I upheld my part of our deal by marrying you and cutting myself off from the world for weeks. I even threw some great sex into the bargain free.'

'Don't do that. Don't negate what we shared over this... This is just—'

'Business?' she finished for him. 'Am I to believe I've crossed the threshold into your personal life now?'

'Could you honestly doubt it?' His eyes seemed so sincere. 'Priya, none of what we shared was a lie. I was too afraid to admit it at the time because...well, because I knew I had messed up. I knew I had to fix this if we had any chance.'

'A chance for what, Eros? For another few weeks of sex until you grow tired of me? You know what? It doesn't matter.'

'Of *course* it matters.' He raised his voice, one hand reaching for her as though he might simply grab her and kiss her into submission. 'Priya, your father's company was just as corrupt as Zeus's. I've been in your position. I found out about my father's corruption and I tried to take him down. Xander stood in my way and I ended up punished severely for my efforts. It almost broke me. I didn't want that kind of pain for you.'

'You could have trusted me to do the right thing. That was my choice to make. How dare you take that from me?' She breathed heavily, feeling despair turn her to ice once more. 'What is to stop me from ending this marriage right now and taking your revenge from you? What have I left to lose?'

He froze, his brows lowering as he nodded once. 'That would be your choice. I wouldn't stand in your way.'

Divorcing now would erase everything, including any claim Eros had on Zeus's empire. Her own inheritance hadn't yet been unlocked either. Without Eros, it would be impossible for her to rectify whatever mess had been made of the firm, but she had already decided she needed to walk away from Davidson Khan once and for all. The evidence that the firm had been built on bad deals and corruption from the start was painful to accept but she could not allow herself to fight for a legacy of lies.

'So that's it?' Eros asked. The rain was plastering his hair to his proud face. 'You've made your decision already? There's no need for me to say my piece?'

'What else is there to say?' She pushed down the sadness at her own words, resisting the urge to listen to his empty defence of actions she could not forgive. To hope that he might not be the cold, calculating bastard she had accused him of being. 'Chalk it up as a bad business venture.'

His head snapped back slightly at her words, his jaw so tight she feared it might break. 'If you walk away from me now, Priya, I won't follow you.'

She felt tears fill her eyes as she nodded once. 'We both know it wouldn't make a difference.'

She began to walk away and stiffened as she felt him move to her side, covering her with his umbrella. She hardly breathed as she lowered herself into the car, every cell of her being screaming at her to forget her pride and common sense. But she knew that was just her broken heart talking and right now she needed her head to stay in control if she had any hope of surviving this.

She looked out at the murky street through the rain on the tinted windows. Eros stood with his hands in his pockets, watching her for a long moment before he turned and walked away.

CHAPTER THIRTEEN

PRIYA ONCE AGAIN stepped into the beautiful building that had once housed Davidson Khan Financial and fought the wave of melancholy that threatened to overtake her. In the week since her world had come crashing down, she had spent sleepless nights trying to come to terms with everything and formulate a new way forward.

Despite the gilded building having been in their family for over a hundred years, her uncle had apparently mortgaged the premises at high cost. The initial papers she had signed to begin divorce proceedings had not affected her inheritance, but it would likely take months for her to have the means to put any kind of stop to the sale. So now the property had been sold at auction and she was being forced to clear out the remnants of memorabilia and private documents before the relevant authorities came and formally repossessed everything.

* * *

Hours passed and she found the work oddly soothing as she sorted through framed photographs of her father on his various charitable projects. Seeing the evidence of his good side did not excuse the bad but she had to find some way to make peace with the memory of the man she'd loved.

The evening light had begun to wane just as she finished packing various files and mementos into boxes. As she looked around the warm wood-panelled walls she felt a lump of emotion in her throat. Who was she, without this as her goal? She had spent so long preparing to step into a place that was now simply…gone. Her investment firm in London had kindly asked her to distance her name from theirs while her uncle's case was still ongoing, so she had begun tentatively considering the possibility of her own start-up. It would be a risk, but she found she had become a little less averse to the idea of an adventure.

Pushing her thoughts away from the image of the man who had brought about so much change in her, she paused as she heard the distinct but distant roar of an engine come to a stop outside. It was Manhattan, of course there were plenty of cars out on the streets, but this was the kind of engine that made her car enthusiast's mind stop and take notice. The kind of vehicle that was usually driven by someone wealthy and powerful.

Her heart skipped a beat and she rushed to the window, looking down to see a sleek red sports car parked out front.

Before she could think through her actions logically, she took the grand polished oak staircase that sloped down to the main entrance of the building. However, it was not Eros who stood in the gleaming parquet foyer but his mother.

She had seen the elegant blonde the week before through the spyhole of her apartment door, hand-delivering the relevant documentation necessary to begin divorce proceedings. She hadn't opened the door. She had signed and returned the forms via courier, knowing that the dissolution would likely not be finalized for months but at least the process had begun.

'Don't worry, I'm not here to cause trouble,' Arista Theodorou said with a smile.

'How did you know to find me here?' Priya frowned.

'I didn't.' The other woman spoke with authority, her eyes moving to take in the details of the space around them. 'I tried your apartment first but you didn't answer so I decided to take a chance. I do hope you haven't cleared everything out already.'

'Why wouldn't I?' Priya crossed her arms over

her chest. 'It's not mine any longer. I don't think it ever was.'

'What if there was a chance to take it back for yourself?'

'I've considered every possibility. I would know if there was one.'

'I'm here on behalf of the person who just bought the building at auction. I've been authorised to sign over the deeds with immediate effect for your purchase. If that's something you would be interested in.'

'Of course it is.' Priya frowned. 'But—'

The older woman cut across her protest with a single raised hand. 'I can expedite the access to your full inheritance, a sizeable amount from my understanding, and the transaction would be done in full.'

'Why would you…?' She paused, realisation dawning. 'Eros sent you.'

'I've begun doing some consultancy work for Arcum. He thought you might take the offer better from someone else.'

Priya turned away, hiding the wave of sadness that came from knowing he had bought the entire building just to give her exclusive access to purchase it herself. A memory rose, unbidden, of lying in his arms as the dawn light filtered through the windows, telling him of all the strategies and ideas she'd had in preparation for taking over the company.

He had been impressed with her ideas, even taking notes to adapt some of his own practices at Arcum. He had called her an innovator. He'd believed in her. No matter what mistakes he had made, she knew that much was true.

Now…she was without any purpose for her innovation. She had no idea who she was.

Arista's heels clicked across the floor, drawing Priya's attention back to the present.

'Was it always a wealth management firm?' she asked, considering one of the ground-floor conference rooms with gleaming oak floors and an impressive antique chandelier.

'The building has been in my family since it was built more than a century ago. They were in the steel business at first, I believe. It's been reinvented a few times since then.'

'Reinvention is good, trust me. I've recently found myself in a similar position. A place like this could provide a very grand landing space for women like me who mostly travel with our work. I don't fancy sharing office space with a bunch of loud digital nomads.' She surveyed the surroundings once more. 'I've been on the hunt for a sophisticated alternative to renting hotel suites.'

Priya felt the suggestion seep into her consciousness. It was a good idea. A great one, even.

She knew she wasn't ready to begin a large business just yet or take on a lot of staff. She wasn't even sure what kind of approach she'd take, with her own name on the door. The idea of starting up shared office space as she began her own company was clever.

'Thank you,' she said, meaning the words.

Arista waved it off. 'It's the least I can do after all the trouble I caused.' The other woman pursed her lips, her eyes darting away for a moment before she finally spoke. 'I assume that Eros has already told you the part I played in everything?'

'He mentioned it.'

'I'd like a chance to explain myself, if I may.' Arista's tone was flat and to the point as she continued, explaining that she had, in fact, been the reason that Eros had even set his sights upon revenge in the first place. She could hear the regret in the older woman's voice and then the anger as she spoke of finding out that Eros had double-crossed her. She apologised, revealing that she had already had an inkling of Vikram's corruption but hadn't realised her influence would become the catalyst behind the investigation into Davidson Khan, which had turned into a runaway train of sorts.

'He should have told me about all of this.' Priya turned to stare out the glass doorway to the lights outside. 'Why didn't he just tell me?

He allowed me to vilify him rather than explain.'
Or had he tried? She thought back to their painful moment on the rain-soaked street. He had
mentioned his mother but she had been too hurt
to hear it.

'He is a very proud man. Always has been.'
Arista shrugged. 'I have treated him poorly in
the past. He was such a sensitive child and I was
a selfish mother. I want to put that right now...if
he'll let me. I always compared him to Zeus but
they are nothing alike.'

'No, they are not,' Priya snapped. 'He is so
much more than anyone believes him to be, and
I include myself in that.'

'Spoken like a woman in love,' Arista said
softly.

Priya fought the sudden emotion clawing at
her throat. 'I do love him. I know that now and
I wish things had been different. But maybe this
is the best way.'

'I had a feeling you might but I wasn't sure...
until you sent me back the divorce papers without your signature on the dotted line.'

'That's impossible. I remember signing them.
I was...' She thought back to that day, sitting
in her apartment and staring at Eros's name on
the white sheets until the tears had eventually
stopped pouring and she'd fallen asleep.

'I have them right here, you can of course sign them right now again. If you actually want to?'

Priya felt an explosion of something dangerously close to hope bloom somewhere in the centre of her chest. She had never been a firm believer in signs or destiny but she had to admit this felt…right.

'If you're about to ask me where he is, technically I'm not supposed to know.' Arista swirled her car keys on one long, slim fingertip. 'But if I *were* the type to keep tabs on my son, I would tell you that he is currently about to board a plane out of the country, never to return.'

'Never to return? But what about Mytikas Holdings?'

'He walked away from all that. He decided he no longer wanted anything to do with Zeus's legacy. He only stayed in town this long to ensure that you got this building. Once he knew that had been done he arranged the first flight out of here.'

Arista took a step towards her, placing her car keys firmly in the centre of Priya's shaking hand. 'The flight leaves in twenty minutes. Go catch your husband.'

Eros stepped onto his jet and took a seat nearest the drinks bar.

The decision to finally leave New York had

not been easy, hence the alcohol. If he hadn't remained slightly drunk for most of the previous week, he probably would have hunted Priya down and forced her to hear him out. But his own pride and the memory of how easily she'd presumed the worst of him still stung. He'd believed they had achieved a level of trust between them. Apparently he'd been wrong.

He'd barely slept in the days it had taken to settle his affairs with Xander and try his best to put things right before he left the country for good. During a single, tense phone call with his brother, he had almost felt compelled to ask how married life was treating him, but the weight of the past was still too heavy between them. Xander hadn't known of Priya's uncle's corruption, just as he hadn't known that Priya had not consented to her uncle's wish to sell. He had seemed genuinely remorseful for the way things had panned out, not that Eros had stayed on the line for very long to chat.

Perhaps one day he might try to mend the relationship with his older brother, but for now, staying anywhere near New York was out of the question. Priya's scent on his sheets had haunted him—even driving past Central Park had made him think of her.

But returning to Myrtus or Halki was equally out of the question. Too many memories. He had settled on the plan to return to Athens first and focus on work, then maybe expand into the Asian market ahead of his original schedule. Yes, Asia sounded ideal, he thought as he downed an entire tumbler of whiskey in one go. Thousands of miles of physical distance seemed necessary when it came to Priya Davidson Khan.

He wondered if she'd got the papers that gave her the right to purchase the Davidson Khan building yet. He knew that in clearing the way for her to gain access to her own fortune, he had completely removed any other need she might have for him. But he had wanted to set her free from their bargain and he just hoped that clearing his own conscience would be enough for him to move on and forget.

It had to be.

'What's taking so long?' he called to the cabin attendant, seeing that the door of the aircraft was still ajar. 'What are we waiting for?'

'We were told to wait for important documentation.' The young man shrugged.

'Told to wait by whom?' Eros frowned, staring out at the busy airport.

It was fast approaching nightfall and a light fog bathed everything in a silvery glow, but as he squinted he could see a set of headlights advancing across the tarmac towards them at high speed. As it came closer, he saw it was a sleek red sports car, not unlike the one his mother drove. In fact, it *was* Arista's car, he realised as the licence plate came into view. Cursing under his breath, Eros clenched his jaw, approached the door of the jet and steeled himself for whatever could possibly have warranted his mother delaying his flight.

But when the door opened and a familiar curvaceous shape emerged, he felt his breath catch. He knew those curves so well he could have picked them out in a darkened room. Priya stepped out into the cold evening air and visibly shivered as a gust of wind sent her hair flying around her face. She wore the remnants of a sleek black suit, seeming to have forgotten to put on whatever blazer or jacket came with it.

'I didn't know if I could make it on time.' She spoke loudly over the hum of the airport around them, biting her lower lip. 'Your mother told me you had walked away from everything, that you were never coming back to New York, and I—'

'Why did Arista come to you? Was there an issue with the building?'

She shook her head, taking a few steps closer. 'No. I own it outright now, just as you arranged. Thank you for that.'

'You came all this way and delayed my flight just to thank me?'

The silence stretched between them but Eros

forced himself to stay still. He had made a fool of himself once, he would not do it again.

'She came to tell me that apparently I failed to sign the divorce papers correctly.' She gestured to the sheaf of papers she held in one hand and moved to the bottom of the steps, looking up at him as she slowly ascended. 'She asked me if I truly wanted to divorce you.'

He could smell the scent of her perfume on the air as she came to a stop a few steps down from him. Her hands seemed to be trembling.

'What did you tell her?' he asked, feeling his heart pound uncomfortably in his chest.

She took a breath, a nervous smile touching the corners of her lips. 'I don't think I actually answered her, now that I think of it. I pretty much just drove straight here. You said you wouldn't follow me…but I don't think I believed you. And now…now you're just leaving?'

'Priya… I couldn't trust myself to even be in the same room to sign my name on the documents that would begin to end this marriage. I wanted to make sure that our union would be dissolved cleanly, without pressure from me. I wanted you to make your own choices.'

'That's the thing.' She shook her head. 'I think, even in all of my anger, I couldn't bear to sign my name on a document that would break my heart even further.'

He felt her words hit him square in the chest. 'I never meant to break your heart. Trust me, if I could have shielded you from the pain of losing the company—'

'It wasn't just sadness about losing the company. I was losing you too.' A sheen of moisture shone in her dark eyes and when her voice broke, Eros felt his body move of its own volition. He was down the steps and holding her in his arms before he had as much as taken a breath.

'Don't,' he rasped. 'I've been trying to do the right thing by leaving you alone. I won't be able to walk away if you're crying. I can't bear it.'

'I don't want you to leave me alone.' She looked up at him, teardrops glistening in her eyelashes. 'I'm sorry that my own fears and anger blinded me to the fact that you were only ever trying to protect me. You said you were a selfish bastard but… I only ever felt cared for when we were together.'

'Priya…' He whispered her name like a prayer, holding her against his chest with so much force he feared he might break her. 'If anyone should apologise, it's me. I may have started out with bad intentions but I assure you my regrets are enough to keep me company for decades. I know that I don't deserve your forgiveness, but it doesn't stop me craving it… It doesn't stop me craving you. I don't deserve you.'

'Don't say that. That's not how love works, Eros. We are both deserving, no matter what mistakes we make.'

He stilled, looking down at her. 'Love?'

Uncertainty marred her brow for a moment before she finally spoke. 'You may have stolen your bride at first, Eros, but I fell in love with you quite willingly. Even this past week when I told myself that it was over... I can't seem to stop loving you.'

'Don't stop. Please, don't stop.' He leaned down, claiming her lips like a drowning man getting his first gasp of air. That's what this woman was to him. Vital. He pulled away after a moment, running his fingers down the silky length of her hair. God, he had missed touching her, holding her, just being near her.

'You aren't panicking? I know how you feel on the subject of love,' she said quickly, running her fingertips in an idle circle over the middle button of his shirt.

'I knew from the first moment that what I felt for you was more than just a passing attraction. But that day on the fishing boat...and then our first night in Halki...' He shook his head, feeling her hands tighten their grip on his shirt. 'It terrified me. You came into my life and tore down every wall I had and reminded me who I truly am. I love you so much it's driven me halfway to madness over the past week to think of my world without you at the heart of it.'

A small sob escaped her lips as she reached up and claimed his lips once more, their kiss becoming something frantic and primal. Like two souls trying to merge into one.

'Does this mean you will stay my wife?' he asked, between kisses. 'Because I'm not opposed to starting from scratch and wooing you all over again.'

She paused, raising one brow. 'I might amend our new terms to include a very romantic, very lavish proposal.'

'I think we need to finalise this negotiation somewhere a little more private, don't you?' he murmured silkily.

Without warning, Eros picked his wife up and climbed the rest of the staircase into the aircraft. She squirmed and kicked in jest, all the while beaming up at him with so much love in her eyes he feared his heart might burst. He smiled back at her, feeling the air crackle around them with something wild and filled with promise.

His lips couldn't seem to release her for more than a second at a time as he navigated the length of the plane. Priya's laugh was like a balm to his soul as their bodies finally landed in a tangle on the lavish bed in the private cabin.

'Are you stealing me away again, Mr Theodorou?' she asked breathlessly.

Eros framed her face in his hands, feeling a rush of emotion so primal it made his throat clench. 'Always, *agape mou*. Always.'

EPILOGUE

EROS GUIDED THE Aqua Hawk into a smooth landing on the water's surface and moved the vessel gently into the island's unusually busy harbour. He frowned as he scanned the dock, noting it was filled with yachts. The Stavros Theodorou Centre for Rehabilitation was into its second year of business now but it still took his breath away every time he returned to see the evidence of his hard work.

Even before he had finished tying off and securing the vessel he heard the sound of a familiar engine descending the hill at speed. His wife was a veritable speed demon.

A soft smile touched his lips as the white Jeep came to a stop and Priya jumped out of the driver's seat. He moved like lightning down the marina and within minutes she was in his embrace.

'Never leave us for that long again.'

'Agreed.'

He breathed in the vanilla scent of her hair,

smoothing his hands down the familiar curves and dips of her body. Long moments were lost as he took her mouth in a deep sensual kiss, showing her exactly how much he had missed her, body and soul.

She tried to move away and with a gentle growl he lifted her legs around his waist, pulling her even closer against him.

'Eros!' she squeaked, and yet she moved herself even tighter in his arms. 'There are people setting up for the charity dinner on the terrace. But, God, I missed you. I missed the quiet of this place but it's not the same without you.'

'I assumed you'd be kept distracted enough.' He raised one brow.

They both smiled knowingly. Her old wish for constant distraction had become a joke between them, because Priya had not set foot in the New York office in more than six months. For a very good reason.

'Where is my other ferocious she-wolf?'

'Sleeping.' Priya smiled, that familiar warmth entering her gaze every time she spoke of their five-month-old daughter Amara. 'The whole family has already arrived, as you can see. Your mother has not let her granddaughter out of her sight and insists on being called Gia-gia now. I think we may have created a monster.'

Eros smiled, glad that he had chosen to invest

time into mending his relationship with Arista. Priya had shown him that sometimes love meant looking past mistakes and choosing forgiveness. It had been tough, but he'd believed in his mother's remorse. They had even scattered Stavros's ashes together here on the island, laying to rest their grief and ill will.

'I'm not quite ready to share you yet,' Eros rasped, running his hands down her sides and pulling her close. Already he could feel himself responding to her. Pregnancy and new parenthood had only seemed to increase the ferocious hunger he felt for his wife. Watching her grow their child and give birth had been the most intense, powerful experience of his life. And all the while she had continued to grow her own empire from the dust of Davidson Khan Financial and make a name for her own small consulting firm and the sophisticated shared work spaces she'd begun to invest in around the globe.

'Always so greedy.' A sparkle of mischief entered Priya's eyes as her gaze moved to where the seaplane still bobbed and swayed against its moorings. 'You know…we never did get around to christening the newest model.'

She took him by the hands and began a slow, seductive walk down the whitewashed pier. One look in her eyes and he knew she was thinking of the jet-black privacy windows and the long bench in the back. He wondered just how many scandalous things they could do in the small block of time they had before they needed to return to the house.

Eros had barely stopped to close the door of the plane behind them before he had her under him. She pulled off her tank top with one smooth movement and spread her knees wide as he settled between her thighs.

'No time for play?' He teased his words against her lips, laughing low in his throat as he felt her hands moving frantically lower on his hips, hurrying him on to what they both needed. There would be plenty of time for slow lovemaking later.

But when he finally slid inside her and felt her warmth surround him, he fell silent and still, needing a moment to simply feel the connection. Priya's eyes held him captivated, the emotion in them echoing the sudden tightness in his chest.

'Every single time...' he said with wonder, capturing her moans with a deep kiss.

He moved slowly at first, wanting to savour having her under him after their time apart, but soon he gave in to the overpowering need to claim, to possess.

Much later, as their guests began to depart, Priya watched as the evening light began to fade over the grounds of their private domain and small lamps lit the place up. The sprawling villa they'd built on the southern end of the island was an ideal base to keep watch on the centre and hold events for their growing charitable organisation, but the farmhouse on Halki was still their true home.

A small cry grabbed her attention and Priya felt a lump in her throat as she watched the man she loved cradling the tiny life they had created together. Amara was the little spark of joy she had never known she was waiting for. Her pregnancy had come as a complete surprise to them both, the result of a much-needed wild weekend spent on the island after months of crazy working hours and very little sleep.

She felt peace spread through her entire being as she watched her husband coo over the difference in his daughter's size, in her expression, delighting in every moment of her upbringing. This was the story they were weaving together, the family that they were building.

He took a step towards her, cradling them both close. A deep rumbling sigh escaped him when their eyes met and she knew that he was feeling exactly the same thing without words passing between them.

This was true happiness, she thought with sudden clarity, just as she had done countless times over the past four years since this man had come into her life. Since she had taken a leap of faith, believing that happy ever after was in her future after all.

She couldn't have picked a more perfect partner for the adventure.

* * * * *

Head over heels for
Stolen in Her Wedding Gown?
You'll love the next story in
The Greeks' Race to the Altar *miniseries,*
coming soon!

Meanwhile, why not explore these other
Amanda Cinelli stories?

The Secret to Marrying Marchesi
One Night with the Forbidden Princess
Claiming His Replacement Queen
The Vows He Must Keep
Returning to Claim His Heir

Available now!